Charles Dickens

Doctor Marigold's Prescriptions, the Extra Christmas

Number of All the Year Round

Charles Dickens

Doctor Marigold's Prescriptions, the Extra Christmas Number of All the Year Round

ISBN/EAN: 9783337384241

Printed in Europe, USA, Canada, Australia, Japan

Cover: Foto ©Andreas Hilbeck / pixelio.de

More available books at **www.hansebooks.com**

DOCTOR MARIGOLD'S PRESCRIPTIONS.

THE EXTRA CHRISTMAS NUMBER OF **ALL THE YEAR ROUND.**

CONDUCTED BY CHARLES DICKENS.

CONTAINING THE AMOUNT OF TWO ORDINARY NUMBERS.

CHRISTMAS, 1865.

Price
4d.

INDEX.

I.

TO BE TAKEN IMMEDIATELY.

I AM a Cheap Jack, and my own father's name was Willum Marigold. It was in his lifetime supposed by some that his name was William, but my own father always consistently said, No, it was Willum. On which point I content myself with looking at the argument this way :—If a man is not allowed to know his own name in a free country, how much is he allowed to know in a land of slavery? As to looking at the argument through the medium of the Register, Willum Marigold come into the world before Registers come up much—and went out of it too. They wouldn't have been greatly in his line neither, if they had chanced to come up before him.

I was born on the Queen's highway, but it was the King's at that time. A doctor was fetched to my own mother by my own father, when it took place on a common; and in consequence of his being a very kind gentleman, and accepting no fee but a tea-tray, I was named Doctor, out of gratitude and compliment to him. There you have me. Doctor Marigold.

I am at present a middle-aged man of a broadish build, in cords, leggings, and a sleeved waistcoat the strings of which is always gone behind. Repair them how you will, they go like fiddle-strings. You have been to the theatre, and you have seen one of the wiolin-players screw up his wiolin, after listening to it as if it had been whispering the secret to him that it feared it was out of order, and then you have heard it snap. That's as exactly similar to my waistcoat, as a waistcoat and a wiolin can be like one another.

I am partial to a white hat, and I like a shawl round my neck wore loose and easy. Sitting down is my favourite posture. If I have a taste in point of personal jewellery, it is mother-of-pearl buttons. There you have me again, as large as life.

The doctor having accepted a tea-tray, you'll guess that my father was a Cheap Jack before me. You are right. He was. It was a pretty tray. It represented a large lady going along a serpentining up-hill gravel-walk, to attend a little church. Two swans had likewise come astray with the same intentions. When I call her a large lady, I don't mean in point of breadth, for there she fell below my views, but she more than made it up in heighth; her heighth and slimness was—in short THE heighth of both.

I often saw that tray, after I was the innocently smiling cause (or more likely screeching one) of the doctor's standing it up on a table against the wall in his consulting-room. Whenever my own father and mother were in that part of the country, I used to put my head (I have heard my own mother say it was flaxen curls at that time, though you wouldn't know an old hearth-broom from it now, till you come to the handle and found it wasn't me) in at the doctor's door, and the doctor was always glad to see me, and said, "Aha, my brother practitioner! Come in, little M.D. How are your inclinations as to sixpence?"

You can't go on for ever, you'll find, nor yet could my father nor yet my mother. If you don't go off as a whole when you are about due, you're liable to go off in part, and two to one your head's the part. Gradually my father went off his, and my mother went off hers. It was in a harmless way, but it put out the family where I boarded them. The old couple, though retired, got to be wholly and solely devoted to the Cheap Jack business, and were always selling the family off. Whenever the cloth was laid for dinner, my father began rattling the plates and dishes, as we do in our line when we put up crockery for a bid, only he had lost the trick of it, and mostly let 'em drop and broke 'em. As the old lady had been used to sit in the cart, and hand the articles out one by one to the old gentleman on the footboard to sell, just in the same way she handed him every item of the family's property, and they disposed of it in their own imaginations from morning to night. At last the old gentleman, lying bedridden in the same room with the old lady, cries out in the old patter, fluent, after having been silent for two days and nights: "Now here, my jolly companions every one—which the Nightingale club in a village was held, At the sign of the Cabbage and Shears, Where the singers no doubt would have greatly excelled, But for want of taste voices and ears—now here, my jolly companions every one, is a working model of a used-up old Cheap Jack, without a tooth in his head, and with a pain in every bone: so like life that it would be just as good if it wasn't better, just as bad if it wasn't worse, and just as new if it wasn't worn out. Bid for the working model of the old Cheap Jack, who has drunk more gunpowder-tea with the ladies in his time than would blow the lid off a washerwoman's copper, and carry it as many thousands of miles higher than the moon as nought nix nought, divided by the national debt, carry nothing to the poor-rates, three under, and two over. Now my hearts of oak and men of straw, what do you say for the lot? Two shillings, a shilling, tenpence, eightpence, sixpence, fourpence. Twopence? Who said twopence? The gentleman in the scarecrow's hat? I am ashamed of the gentleman in the scarecrow's hat. I really am ashamed of him for his want of public spirit. Now I'll tell you what I'll do with you. Come! I'll throw you in a working model of a old woman that was married to the old Cheap Jack so long ago, that upon my word and honour it took place in Noah's Ark, before the Unicorn could get in to forbid the banns by blowing a tune upon his horn. There now! Come! What do you say for both? I'll tell you what I'll do with you. I don't bear you malice for being so backward. Here! If you make me a bid that'll only reflect a little credit on your town, I'll throw you in a warming-pan for nothing, and lend you a toasting-fork for life. Now come; what do you say after that splendid offer? Say two pound, say thirty shillings, say a pound, say ten shillings, say five, say two and six. You don't say even two and six? You say two and three? No. You shan't have the lot for two and three. I'd sooner give it you, if you was good looking enough. Here! Missis! Chuck the old man and woman into the cart, put the horse to, and drive 'em away and bury 'em!" Such were the last words of Willum Marigold, my own father, and they were carried out, by him and by his wife my own mother on one and the same day, as I ought to know, having followed as mourner.

My father had been a lovely one in his time at the Cheap Jack work, as his dying observations went to prove. But I top him. I don't say it because it's myself, but because it has been universally acknowledged by all that has had the means of comparison. I have worked at it. I have measured myself against other public speakers, Members of Parliament, Platforms, Pulpits, Counsel learned in the law—and where I have found 'em good, I have took a bit of imitation from 'em, and where I have found 'em bad, I have let 'em, alone. Now I'll tell you what. I mean to go down into my grave declaring that of all the callings ill used in Great Britain, the Cheap Jack calling is the worst used. Why ain't we a profession? Why ain't we endowed with privileges? Why are we forced to take out a hawkers' license, when no such thing is expected of the political hawkers? Where's the difference betwixt us? Except that we are Cheap Jacks and they are Dear Jacks, I don't see any difference but what's in our favour.

For look here! Say it's election-time. I am on the footboard of my cart in the market-place on a Saturday night. I put up a general miscellaneous lot. I say: "Now here my free and independent woters, I'm a going to give you such a chance as you never had in all your born days, nor yet the days preceding. Now I'll show you what I am a going to do with you. Here's a pair of razors that'll shave you closer than the Board of Guardians, here's a flat-iron worth its weight in gold, here's a frying-pan artificially flavoured with essence of beefsteaks to that degree that you've only got for the rest of your lives to fry bread and dripping in it and there you are replete with animal food, here's a genuine chronometer watch in such a solid silver case that you may knock at the door with it when you come home late from a social meeting and rouse your wife and family and save up your knocker for the postman, and here's half a dozen dinner plates that you may play the cymbals with to charm the baby when it's fractious. Stop! I'll throw you in another article and I'll give you that, and it's a rolling-pin, and if the baby can only get it well into its mouth when its teeth is coming and rub the gums once with it, they'll come through double, in a fit of laughter equal to being tickled. Stop again! I'll throw you in another article, because I don't like the looks of you, for you haven't the appearance of buyers unless I lose by you, and because I'd rather lose than not take money to-night, and that's a looking-glass in which you may see how ugly you look when you don't bid. What do you say now? Come! Do you say a pound? Not you, for you haven't got it. Do you say ten shillings? Not you, for you owe more to the tallyman. Well then, I'll tell you what I'll do with you. I'll heap 'em all on the footboard of the cart—there they are! razors, flat-iron, frying-pan, chronometer watch, dinner plates, rolling-pin, and looking-glass—take 'em all away for four shillings, and I'll give you sixpence for your trouble!" This is me, the Cheap Jack. But on the Monday morning, in the same market-place, comes the Dear Jack on the hustings—his cart—and what does he say? "Now my free and independent woters, I am a going to give you such a chance" (he begins just like me) "as you never had in all your born days, and that's the chance of sending Myself to Parliament. Now I'll tell you what I am a going to do for you. Here's the interests of this magnificent town promoted above all the rest of the civilised and uncivilised earth. Here's your railways carried, and your neighbours' railways jockeyed. Here's all your sons in the Post-office. Here's Britannia smiling on you. Here's the eyes of Europe on you. Here's uniwersal prosperity for you, repletion of animal food, golden corn-fields, gladsome homesteads, and rounds of applause from your own hearts, all in one lot and that's myself. Will you take me as I stand? You won't? Well then, I'll tell you what I'll do with you. Come now! I'll throw you in anything you ask for. There! Church-rates, abolition of church-rates, more malt tax, no malt tax, uniwersal education to the highest mark or uniwersal ignorance to the lowest, total abolition of flogging in the army or a dozen for every private once a month all round, Wrongs of Men or Rights of Women,—only say which it shall be, take 'em or leave 'em, and I'm of your opinion altogether, and the lot's your own on your own terms. There! You won't take it yet? Well then, I'll tell you what I'll do with you. Come! You *are* such free and independent woters, and I *am* so proud of you—you *are* such a noble and enlightened constituency, and I *am* so ambitious of the honour and dignity of being your member, which is by far the highest level to which the wings of the human mind can soar—that I'll tell you what I'll do with you. I'll throw you in all the public-houses in your magnificent town for nothing. Will that content you? It won't? You won't take the lot yet? Well then, before I put the horse in and drive away, and make the offer to the next most magnificent town that can be discovered, I'll tell you what I'll do. Take the lot, and I'll drop two thousand pound in the streets of your magnificent town for them to pick up that can. Not enough? Now look here. This is the very furthest that I'm a going to. I'll make it two thousand five hundred. And still you won't? Here, missis! Put the horse—no, stop half a moment, I shouldn't like to turn my back upon you neither for a trifle, I'll make it two thousand seven hundred and fifty pound. There! Take the lot on your own terms, and I'll count out two thousand seven hundred and fifty pound on the footboard of the cart, to be dropped in the streets of your magnificent town for them to pick up that can. What do you say? Come now! You won't do better, and you may do worse. You take it? Hooray! Sold again, and got the seat!"

These Dear Jacks soap the people shameful, but we Cheap Jacks don't. We tell 'em the truth about themselves to their faces, and scorn to court 'em. As to wenturesomeness in the way of puffing up the lots, the Dear Jacks beat us hollow. It is considered in the Cheap Jack calling that better patter can be made out of a gun than any article we put up from the cart, except a pair of spectacles. I often hold forth about a gun for a quarter of an hour, and feel as if I need never leave off. But when I tell 'em what the gun can do, and what the gun has brought down, I never go half so far as the Dear Jacks do when they make speeches in praise of *their* guns—their great guns that set 'em on to do it. Besides, I'm in business for myself, I ain't sent down into the market-place to order, as they are. Besides again, my guns don't know what I say in their laudation, and their guns do, and the whole concern of 'em have reason to be sick and ashamed all round. These are some of my arguments for declaring that the Cheap Jack calling is treated ill in Great Britain, and for turning warm when I think of the other Jacks in question setting themselves up to pretend to look down upon it.

I courted my wife from the footboard of the cart. I did indeed. She was a Suffolk young woman, and it was in Ipswich market-place right opposite the corn-chandler's shop. I had noticed her up at a window last Saturday that was, appreciating highly. I had took to her, and I had said to myself, "If not already disposed of, I'll have that lot." Next Saturday that come, I pitched the cart on the same pitch, and I was in very high feather indeed, keeping 'em laughing the whole of the time and getting off the goods briskly. At last I took out of my waistcoat-pocket, a small lot wrapped in soft paper, and I put it this way (looking up at the window where she was). "Now here my blooming English maidens is an article, the last article of the present evening's sale, which I offer to only you the lovely Suffolk Dumplings biling over with beauty, and I won't take a bid of a thousand pound for, from any man alive. Now what is it? Why, I'll tell you what it is. It's made of fine gold, and it's not broke though there's a hole in the middle of it, and it's stronger than any fetter that ever was forged, though it's smaller than any finger in my set of ten. Why ten? Because when my parents made over my property to me, I tell you true, there was twelve sheets, twelve towels, twelve table-cloths, twelve knives, twelve forks, twelve table-spoons, and twelve teaspoons, but my set of fingers was two short of a dozen and could never since be matched. Now what else is it? Come I'll tell you. It's a hoop of solid gold, wrapped in a silver curl-paper that I myself took off the shining locks of the ever beautiful old lady in Threadneedle-street, London city. I wouldn't tell you so if I hadn't the paper to show, or you mightn't believe it even of me. Now what else is it? It's a man-trap and a handcuff, the parish stocks and a leg-lock, all in gold and all in one. Now what else is it? It's a wedding ring. Now I'll tell you what I'm a-going to do with it. I'm not a-going to offer this lot for money, but I mean to give it to the next of you beauties that laughs, and I'll pay her a visit to-morrow morning at exactly half after nine o'clock as the chimes go, and I'll take her out for a walk to put up the banns." *She* laughed, and got the ring handed up to her. When I called in the morning, she says, "Oh dear! It's never you and you never mean it?" "It's ever me," says I, "and I am ever yours, and I ever mean it." So we got married, after being put up three times—which, by-the-by, is quite in the Cheap Jack way again, and shows once more how the Cheap Jack customs pervade society.

She wasn't a bad wife, but she had a temper. If she could have parted with that one article at a sacrifice, I wouldn't have swopped her away in exchange for any other woman in England. Not that I ever did swop her away, for we lived together till she died, and that was thirteen year. Now my lords and ladies and gentle-folks all, I'll let you into a secret, though you won't believe it. Thirteen year of temper in a Palace would try the worst of you, but thir-teen year of temper in a Cart would try the best of you. You are kept so very close to it in a cart, you see. There's thousands of couples among you, getting on like sweet ile upon a whetstone in houses five and six pairs of stairs high, that would go to the Divorce Court in a cart. Whether the jolting makes it worse, I don't undertake to decide, but in a cart it does come home to you and stick to you. Wiolence in a cart is so wiolent, and aggrawation in a cart is so aggrawating.

We might have had such a pleasant life! A roomy cart, with the large goods hung outside and the bed slung underneath it when on the road, an iron pot and a kettle, a fireplace for the cold weather, a chimney for the smoke, a hang-ing shelf and a cupboard, a dog, and a horse. What more do you want? You draw off upon a bit of turf in a green lane or by the roadside, you hobble your old horse and turn him grazing, you light your fire upon the ashes of the last visitors, you cook your stew, and you wouldn't call the Emperor of France your father. But have a temper in the cart, flinging language and the hardest goods in stock at you, and where are you then? Put a name to your feelings.

My dog knew as well when she was on the turn as I did. Before she broke out, he would give a howl, and bolt. How he knew it, was a mystery to me, but the sure and certain know-ledge of it would wake him up out of his soundest sleep, and he would give a howl, and bolt. At such times I wished I was him.

The worst of it was, we had a daughter born to us, and I love children with all my heart. When she was in her furies, she beat the child. This got to be so shocking as the child got to be four or five year old, that I have many a time gone on with my whip over my shoulder, at the old horse's head, sobbing and crying worse than ever little Sophy did. For how could I prevent it? Such a thing is not to be tried with such a temper—in a cart—with-out coming to a fight. It's in the natural size and formation of a cart to bring it to a fight. And then the poor child got worse terrified than before, as well as worse hurt generally, and her mother made complaints to the next people we lighted on, and the word went round, "Here's a wretch of a Cheap Jack been a beating his wife."

Little Sophy was such a brave child! She grew to be quite devoted to her poor father, though he could do so little to help her. She had a wonderful quantity of shining dark hair, all curling natural about her. It is quite asto-nishing to me now, that I didn't go tearing mad when I used to see her run from her mother before the cart, and her mother catch her by this hair, and pull her down by it, and beat her. Such a brave child I said she was. Ah! with reason.

"Don't you mind next time, father dear," she would whisper to me, with her little face still flushed, and her bright eyes still wet; "if I don't cry out, you may know I am not much hurt. And even if I do cry out, it will only be to get mother to let go and leave off." What I have seen the little spirit bear—for me—without crying out!

Yet in other respects her mother took great care of her. Her clothes were always clean and neat, and her mother was never tired of working at 'em. Such is the inconsistency in things. Our being down in the marsh country in un-healthy weather, I consider the cause of Sophy's taking bad low fever; but however she took it, once she got it she turned away from her mother for evermore, and nothing would per-suade her to be touched by her mother's hand. She would shiver and say "No, no, no," when it was offered at, and would hide her face on my shoulder, and hold me tighter round the neck.

The Cheap Jack business had been worse than ever I had known it, what with one thing and what with another (and not least what with railroads, which will cut it all to pieces, I ex-pect at last), and I was run dry of money. For which reason, one night at that period of little Sophy's being so bad, either we must have come to a dead-lock for victuals and drink, or I must have pitched the cart as I did.

I couldn't get the dear child to lie down or leave go of me, and indeed I hadn't the heart to try, so I stepped out on the footboard with her holding round my neck. They all set up a laugh when they see us, and one chuckle-headed Joskin (that I hated for it) made the bidding, "tuppence for her!"

"Now, you country boobies," says I, feeling as if my heart was a heavy weight at the end of a broken sash-line, "I give you notice that I am a going to charm the money out of your pockets, and to give you so much more than your money's worth that you'll only persuade yourselves to draw your Saturday night's wages ever again arterwards, by the hopes of meeting me to lay 'em out with, which you never will, and why not? Because I've made my fortune by selling my goods on a large scale for seventy-five per cent less than I give for 'em, and I am consequently to be elevated to the House of Peers next week, by the title of the Duke of Cheap and Markis Jackaloorul. Now let's know what you want to-night, and you shall have it. But first of all, shall I tell you why I have got this little girl round my neck? You don't want to know? Then you shall. She belongs to the Fairies.

She's a fortune-teller. She can tell me all about you in a whisper, and can put me up to whether you're a-going to buy a lot or leave it. Now do you want a saw? No, she says you don't, because you're too clumsy to use one. Else here's a saw which would be a lifelong blessing to a handy man, at four shillings, at three and six, at three, at two and six, at two, at eighteenpence. But none of you shall have it at any price, on account of your well-known awkwardness which would make it manslaughter. The same objection applies to this set of three planes which I won't let you have neither, so don't bid for 'em. Now I am a-going to ask her what you do want. (Then I whispered, "Your head burns so, that I am afraid it hurts you bad, my pet," and she answered, without opening her heavy eyes, "Just a little, father.") Oh! This little fortune-teller says it's a memorandum-book you want. Then why didn't you mention it? Here it is. Look at it. Two hundred super-fine hot-pressed wire-wove pages—if you don't believe me, count 'em—ready ruled for your expenses, an everlastingly-pointed pencil to put 'em down with, a double-bladed penknife to scratch 'em out with, a book of printed tables to calculate your income with, and a camp-stool to sit down upon while you give your mind to it! Stop! And an umbrella to keep the moon off when you give your mind to it on a pitch dark night. Now I won't ask you how much for the lot, but how little? How little are you thinking of? Don't be ashamed to mention it, because my fortune-teller knows already. (Then making believe to whisper, I kissed her, and she kissed me.) Why, she says you're thinking of as little as three and threepence! I couldn't have believed it, even of you, unless she told me. Three and threepence! And a set of printed tables in the lot that'll calculate your income up to forty thousand a year! With an income of forty thousand a year, you grudge three and sixpence. Well then, I'll tell you my opinion. I so despise the threepence, that I'd sooner take three shillings. There. For three shillings, three shillings, three shillings! Gone. Hand 'em over to the lucky man."

As there had been no bid at all, everybody looked about and grinned at everybody, while I touched little Sophy's face and asked her if she felt faint or giddy. "Not very, father. It will soon be over." Then turning from the pretty patient eyes, which were opened now, and seeing nothing but grins across my lighted grease-pot, I went on again in my Cheap Jack style. "Where's the butcher?" (My sorrowful eye had just caught sight of a fat young butcher on the outside of the crowd.) She says the good luck is the butcher's. "Where is he?" Everybody handed on the blushing butcher to the front, and there was a roar, and the butcher felt himself obliged to put his hand in his pocket and take the lot. The party so picked out, in general does feel obliged to take the lot—good four times out of six. Then we had another lot the counterpart of that one, and sold it sixpence cheaper, which is always

wery much enjoyed. Then we had the spectacles. It ain't a special profitable lot, but I put 'em on, and I see what the Chancellor of the Exchequer is going to take off the taxes, and I see what the sweetheart of the young woman in the shawl is doing at home, and I see what the Bishops has got for dinner, and a deal more that seldom fails to fetch 'em up in their spirits; and the better their spirits, the better their bids. Then we had the ladies' lot—the teapot, tea-caddy, glass sugar basin, half a dozen spoons, and caudle-cup—and all the time I was making similar excuses to give a look or two and say a word or two to my poor child. It was while the second ladies' lot was holding 'em enchained that I felt her lift herself a little on my shoulder, to look across the dark street. "What troubles you, darling?" "Nothing troubles me, father. I am not at all troubled. But don't I see a pretty churchyard over there?" "Yes, my dear." "Kiss me twice, dear father, and lay me down to rest upon that churchyard grass so soft and green." I staggered back into the cart with her head dropped on my shoulder, and I says to her mother, "Quick. Shut the door! Don't let those laughing people see!" "What's the matter?" she cries. "O, woman, woman," I tells her, "you'll never catch my little Sophy by her hair again, for she has flown away from you!"

Maybe those were harder words than I meant 'em, but from that time forth my wife took to brooding, and would sit in the cart or walk beside it, hours at a stretch, with her arms crossed and her eyes looking on the ground. When her furies took her (which was rather seldomer than before) they took her in a new way, and she banged herself about to that extent that I was forced to hold her. She got none the better for a little drink now and then, and through some years I used to wonder as I plodded along at the old horse's head whether there was many carts upon the road that held so much dreariness as mine, for all my being looked up to as the King of the Cheap Jacks. So sad our lives went on till one summer evening, when as we were coming into Exeter out of the further West of England, we saw a woman beating a child in a cruel manner, who screamed, "Don't beat me! O mother, mother, mother!" Then my wife stopped her ears and ran away like a wild thing, and next day she was found in the river.

Me and my dog were all the company left in the cart now, and the dog learned to give a short bark when they wouldn't bid, and to give another and a nod of his head when I asked him: "Who said half-a-crown? Are you the gentleman, sir, that offered half-a-crown?" He attained to an immense heighth of popularity, and I shall always believe taught himself entirely out of his own head to growl at any person in the crowd that bid as low as sixpence. But he got to be well on in years, and one night when I was convulsing York with the spectacles, he took a convulsion on his own account upon the very footboard by me, and it finished him.

Being naturally of a tender turn, I had dreadful lonely feelings on me arter this. I conquered 'em at selling times, having a reputation to keep (not to mention keeping myself), but they got me down in private and rolled upon me. That's often the way with us public characters. See us on the footboard, and you'd give pretty well anything you possess to be us. See us off the footboard, and you'd add a trifle to be off your bargain. It was under those circumstances that I come acquainted with a giant. I might have been too high to fall into conversation with him, had it not been for my lonely feelings. For the general rule is, going round the country, to draw the line at dressing up. When a man can't trust his getting a living to his undisguised abilities, you consider him below your sort. And this giant when on view figured as a Roman.

He was a languid young man, which I attribute to the distance betwixt his extremities. He had a little head and less in it, he had weak eyes and weak knees, and altogether you couldn't look at him without feeling that there was greatly too much of him both for his joints and his mind. But he was an amiable though timid young man (his mother let him out, and spent the money), and we come acquainted when he was walking to ease the horse betwixt two fairs. He was called Rinaldo di Velasco, his name being Pickleson.

This giant otherwise Pickleson mentioned to me under the seal of confidence, that beyond his being a burden to himself, his life was made a burden to him, by the cruelty of his master towards a step-daughter who was deaf and dumb. Her mother was dead, and she had no living soul to take her part, and was used most hard. She travelled with his master's caravan only because there was nowhere to leave her, and this giant otherwise Pickleson did go so far as to believe that his master often tried to lose her. He was such a very languid young man, that I don't know how long it didn't take him to get this story out, but it passed through his defective circulation to his top extremity in course of time.

When I heard this account from the giant otherwise Pickleson, and likewise that the poor girl had beautiful long dark hair, and was often pulled down by it and beaten, I couldn't see the giant through what stood in my eyes. Having wiped 'em, I give him sixpence (for he was kept as short as he was long), and he laid it out in two threepennorths of gin-and-water, which so brisked him up, that he sang the Favourite Comic of Shivery Shakey, ain't it cold. A popular effect which his master had tried every other means to get out of him as a Roman, wholly in vain.

His master's name was Mim, a wery hoarse man and I knew him to speak to. I went to that Fair as a mere civilian, leaving the cart outside the town, and I looked about the back of the Vans while the performing was going on, and at last sitting dozing against a muddy cartwheel, I come upon the poor girl who was deaf and dumb. At the first look I might almost have judged that she had escaped from the Wild Beast Show, but at the second I thought better of her, and thought that if she was more cared for and more kindly used she would be like my child. She was just the same age that my own daughter would have been, if her pretty head had not fell down upon my shoulder that unfortunate night.

To cut it short, I spoke confidential to Mim while he was beating the gong outside betwixt two lots of Pickleson's publics, and I put it to him, "She lies heavy on your own hands; what'll you take for her?" Mim was a most ferocious swearer. Suppressing that part of his reply, which was much the longest part, his reply was, "A pair of braces." "Now I'll tell you," says I, "what I'm a going to do with you. I'm a going to fetch you half a dozen pair of the primest braces in the cart, and then to take her away with me." Says Mim (again ferocious), "I'll believe it when I've got the goods, and no sooner." I made all the haste I could, lest he should think twice of it, and the bargain was completed, which Pickleson he was thereby so relieved in his mind that he come out at his little back door, longways like a serpent, and give us Shivery Shakey in a whisper among the wheels at parting.

It was happy days for both of us when Sophy and me began to travel in the cart. I at once give her the name of Sophy, to put her ever towards me in the attitude of my own daughter. We soon made out to begin to understand one another through the goodness of the Heavens, when she knowed that I meant true and kind by her. In a very little time she was wonderful fond of me. You have no idea what it is to have anybody wonderful fond of you, unless you have been got down and rolled upon by the lonely feelings that I have mentioned as having once got the better of me.

You'd have laughed—or the reverse—it's according to your disposition—if you could have seen me trying to teach Sophy. At first I was helped — you'd never guess by what — milestones. I got some large alphabets in a box, all the letters separate on bits of bone, and say we was going to WINDSOR, I give her those letters in that order, and then at every milestone I showed her those same letters in that same order again, and pointed towards the abode of royalty. Another time I give her C A R T, and then chalked the same upon the cart. Another time I give her D O C T O R M A R I G O L D, and hung a corresponding inscription outside my waistcoat. People that met us might stare a bit and laugh, but what did I care if she caught the idea? She caught it after long patience and trouble, and then we did begin to get on swimmingly, I believe you! At first she was a little given to consider me the cart, and the cart the abode of royalty, but that soon wore off.

We had our signs, too, and they was hundreds in number. Sometimes, she would sit looking at me and considering hard how to communicate with me about something fresh—how to ask me what she wanted explained—and then she was (or I thought she was; what does it signify?) so like my child with those years added to her, that I half believed it was herself, trying to tell me where she had been to up in the skies, and what she had seen since that unhappy night when she flied away. She had a pretty face, and now that there was no one to drag at her bright dark hair and it was all in order, there was a something touching in her looks that made the cart most peaceful and most quiet, though not at all melancolly. [N.B. In the Cheap Jack patter, we generally sound it, lemonjolly, and it gets a laugh.]

The way she learnt to understand any look of mine was truly surprising. When I sold of a night, she would sit in the cart unseen by them outside, and would give a eager look into my eyes when I looked in, and would hand me straight the precise article or articles I wanted. And then she would clap her hands and laugh for joy. And as for me, seeing her so bright, and remembering what she was when I first lighted on her, starved and beaten and ragged, leaning asleep against the muddy cart-wheel, it give me such heart that I gained a greater heighth of reputation than ever, and I put Pickleson down (by the name of Mim's Travelling Giant otherwise Pickleson) for a fypunnote in my will.

This happiness went on in the cart till she was sixteen year old. By which time I began to feel not satisfied that I had done my whole duty by her, and to consider that she ought to have better teaching than I could give her. It drew a many tears on both sides when I commenced explaining my views to her, but what's right is right and you can't neither by tears nor laughter do away with its character.

So I took her hand in mine, and I went with her one day to the Deaf and Dumb Establishment in London, and when the gentleman come to speak to us, I says to him: "Now I'll tell you what I'll do with you sir. I am nothing but a Cheap Jack, but of late years I have laid by for a rainy day notwithstanding. This is my only daughter (adopted) and you can't produce a deafer nor a dumber. Teach her the most that can be taught her, in the shortest separation that can be named—state the figure for it—and I am game to put the money down. I won't bate you a single farthing sir but I'll put down the money here and now, and I'll thankfully throw you in a pound to take it. There!" The gentleman smiled, and then, "Well, well," says he, "I must first know what she has learnt already. How do you communicate with her?" Then I showed him, and she wrote in printed writing many names of things and so forth, and we held some sprightly conversation, Sophy and me, about a little story in a book which the gentleman showed her and which she was able to read. "This is most extraordinary," says the gentleman; "is it possible that you have been her only teacher?" "I have been her only teacher, sir," I says, "besides herself." "Then," says the gentleman, and more acceptable words was

never spoke to me, "you're a clever fellow, and a good fellow." This he makes known to Sophy, who kisses his hands, claps her own, and laughs and cries upon it.

We saw the gentleman four times in all, and when he took down my name and asked how in the world it ever chanced to be Doctor, it come out that he was own nephew by the sister's side, if you'll believe me, to the very Doctor that I was called after. This made our footing still easier, and he says to me:

"Now Marigold, tell me what more do you want your adopted daughter to know?"

"I want her sir to be cut off from the world as little as can be, considering her deprivations, and therefore to be able to read whatever is wrote, with perfect ease and pleasure."

"My good fellow," urges the gentleman, opening his eyes wide, "why I can't do that myself!"

I took his joke and give him a laugh (knowing by experience how flat you fall without it) and I mended my words accordingly.

"What do you mean to do with her afterwards?" asks the gentleman, with a sort of a doubtful eye. "To take her about the country?"

"In the cart sir, but only in the cart. She will live a private life, you understand, in the cart. I should never think of bringing her infirmities before the public. I wouldn't make a show of her, for any money."

The gentleman nodded and seemed to approve.

"Well," says he, "can you part with her for two years?"

"To do her that good—yes, sir."

"There's another question," says the gentleman, looking towards her: "Can she part with you for two years?"

I don't know that it was a harder matter of itself (for the other was hard enough to me), but it was harder to get over. However, she was pacified to it at last, and the separation betwixt us was settled. How it cut up both of us when it took place, and when I left her at the door in the dark of an evening, I don't tell. But I know this:—remembering that night, I shall never pass that same establishment without a heart-ache and a swelling in the throat, and I couldn't put you up the best of lots in sight of it with my usual spirit—no, not even the gun, nor the pair of spectacles—for five hundred pound reward from the Secretary of State for the Home Department, and throw in the honour of putting my legs under his mahogany arterwards.

Still, the loneliness that followed in the cart was not the old loneliness, because there was a term put to it however long to look forward to, and because I could think, when I was anyways down, that she belonged to me and I belonged to her. Always planning for her coming back, I bought in a few months' time another cart, and what do you think I planned to do with it? I'll tell you. I planned to fit it up with shelves, and books for her reading, and to have a seat in it where I could sit and see her read, and think that I had been her first teacher.

Not hurrying over the job, I had the fittings knocked together in contriving ways under my own inspection, and here was her bed in a berth with curtains, and there was her reading-table, and here was her writing-desk, and elsewhere was her books in rows upon rows, picters and no picters, bindings and no bindings, gilt-edged and plain, just as I could pick 'em up for her in lots up and down the country, North and South and West and East, Winds liked best and winds liked least, Here and there and gone astray, Over the hills and far away. And when I had got together pretty well as many books as the cart would neatly hold, a new scheme come into my head which, as it turned out, kept my time and attention a good deal employed and helped me over the two years stile.

Without being of an awaricious temper, I like to be the owner of things. I should'nt wish, for instance, to go partners with yourself in the Cheap Jack cart. It's not that I mistrust you, but that I'd rather know it was mine. Similarly, very likely you'd rather know it was yours. Well! A kind of a jealousy began to creep into my mind when I reflected that all those books would have been read by other people long before they was read by her. It seemed to take away from her being the owner of 'em like. In this way, the question got into my head:—Couldn't I have a book new-made express for her, which she should be the first to read?

It pleased me, that thought did, and as I never was a man to let a thought sleep (you must wake up all the whole family of thoughts you've got and burn their nightcaps, or you won't do in the cheap Jack line), I set to work at it. Considering that I was in the habit of changing so much about the country, and that I should have to find out a literary character here to make a deal with, and another literary character there to make a deal with, as opportunities presented, I hit on the plan that this same book should be a general miscellaneous lot—like the razors, flat-iron, chronometer watch, dinner plates, rolling-pin, and looking-glass—and shouldn't be offered as a single individual article like the spectacles or the gun. When I had come to that conclusion, I come to another, which shall likewise be yours.

Often had I regretted that she never had heard me on the footboard, and that she never could hear me. It ain't that *I* am vain, but that *you* don't like to put your own light under a bushel. What's the worth of your reputation, if you can't convey the reason for it to the person you most wish to value it? Now I'll put it to you. Is it worth sixpence, fippence, fourpence, threepence, twopence, a penny, a halfpenny, a farthing? No, it ain't. Not worth a farthing. Very well then. My conclusion was, that I would begin her book with some account of myself. So that, through reading a specimen or two of me on the footboard, she might form an idea of my merits there. I was aware that I couldn't do myself

justice. A man can't write his eye (at least *I* don't know how to), nor yet can a man write his voice, nor the rate of his talk, nor the quickness of his action, nor his general spicy way. But he can write his turns of speech, when he is a public speaker — and indeed I have heard that he very often does, before he speaks 'em.

Well! Having formed that resolution, then come the question of a name. How did I hammer that hot iron into shape? This way. The most difficult explanation I had ever had with her was, how I come to be called Doctor, and yet was no Doctor. After all, I felt that I had failed of getting it correctly into her mind, with my utmost pains. But trusting to her improvement in the two years, I thought that I might trust to her understanding it when she should come to read it as put down by my own hand. Then I thought I would try a joke with her and watch how it took, by which of itself I might fully judge of her understanding it. We had first discovered the mistake we had dropped into, through her having asked me to prescribe for her when she had supposed me to be a Doctor in a medical point of view, so thinks I, " Now, if I give this book the name of my Prescriptions, and if she catches the idea that my only Prescriptions are for her amusement and interest — to make her laugh in a pleasant way, or to make her cry in a pleasant way—it will be a delightful proof to both of us that we have got over our difficulty. It fell out to absolute perfection. For when she saw the book, as I had it got up—the printed and pressed book—lying on her desk in her cart, and saw the title, DOCTOR MARIGOLD'S PRESCRIPTIONS, she looked at me for a moment with astonishment, then fluttered the leaves, then broke out a laughing in the charmingest way, then felt her pulse and shook her head, then turned the pages pretending to read them most attentive, then kissed the book to me, and put it to her bosom with both her hands. I never was better pleased in all my life!

But let me not anticipate. (I take that expression out of a lot of romances I bought for her. I never opened a single one of 'em—and I have opened many—but I found the romancer saying "let me not anticipate." Which being so, I wonder why he did anticipate, or who asked him to it.) Let me not, I say, anticipate. This same book took up all my spare time. It was no play to get the other articles together in the general miscellaneous lot, but when it come to my own article! There! I couldn't have believed the blotting, nor yet the buckling to at it, nor the patience over it. Which again is like the footboard. The public have no idea.

At last it was done, and the two years' time was gone after all the other time before it, and where it's all gone to, Who knows? The new cart was finished—yellow outside, relieved with wer-million and brass fittings—the old horse was put in it, a new 'un and a boy being laid on for the Cheap Jack cart—and I cleaned myself up to go and fetch her. Bright cold weather it was, cart-chimneys smoking, carts pitched private on a piece of waste ground over at Wandsworth where you may see 'em from the Sou' Western Railway when not upon the road. (Look out of the right-hand window going down.)

"Marigold," says the gentleman, giving his hand hearty, "I am very glad to see you."

"Yet I have my doubts, sir," says I, "if you can be half as glad to see me, as I am to see you."

"The time has appeared so long; has it, Marigold?"

"I won't say that, sir, considering its real length; but——"

"What a start, my good fellow!"

Ah! I should think it was! Grown such a woman, so pretty, so intelligent, so expressive! I knew then that she must be really like my child, or I could never have known her, standing quiet by the door.

"You are affected," says the gentleman in a kindly manner.

"I feel, sir," says I, "that I am but a rough chap in a sleeved waistcoat."

"I feel," says the gentleman, "that it was you who raised her from misery and degradation, and brought her into communication with her kind. But why do we converse alone together, when we can converse so well with her? Address her in your own way."

"I am such a rough chap in a sleeved waistcoat, sir," says I, "and she is such a graceful woman, and she stands so quiet at the door!"

"Try if she moves at the old sign," says the gentleman.

They had got it up together o' purpose to please me! For when I give her the old sign, she rushed to my feet, and dropped upon her knees, holding up her hands to me with pouring tears of love and joy; and when I took her hands and lifted her, she clasped me round the neck and lay there; and I don't know what a fool I didn't make of myself, until we all three settled down into talking without sound, as if there was a something soft and pleasant spread over the whole world for us.

Now I'll tell you what I am a going to do with you. I am a going to offer you the general miscellaneous lot, her own book, never read by anybody else but me, added to and completed by me after her first reading of it, eight-and-forty printed pages, six-and-ninety columns, Whiting's own work, Beaufort House to wit, thrown off by the steam-ingine, best of paper, beautiful green wrapper, folded like clean linen come home from the clear-starcher's, and so exquisitely stitched that, regarded as a piece of needlework alone it's better than the sampler of a seamstress undergoing a Competitive Examination for Starvation before the Civil Service Commissioners—and I offer the lot for what? For eight pound? Not so much. For six pound? Less. For four pound?

Why, I hardly expect you to believe me, but that's the sum. Four pound! The stitching alone cost half as much again. Here's forty-eight original pages, ninety-six original columns, for four pound. You want more for the money? Take it. Three whole pages of advertisements of thrilling interest thrown in for nothing. Read 'em and believe 'em. More? My best of wishes for your merry Christmases and your happy New Years, your long lives and your true prosperities. Worth twenty pound good if they are delivered as I send them. Remember! Here's a final prescription added, "To be taken for life," which will tell you how the cart broke down, and where the journey ended. You think Four Pound too much? And still you think so? Come! I'll tell you what then. Say Four Pence, and keep the secret.

II.

NOT TO BE TAKEN AT BED-TIME.

This is the legend of a house called the Devil's Inn, standing in the heather on the top of the Connemara mountains, in a shallow valley hollowed between five peaks. Tourists sometimes come in sight of it on September evenings; a crazy and weather-stained apparition, with the sun glaring at it angrily between the hills, and striking its shattered window-panes. Guides are known to shun it, however.

The house was built by a stranger, who came no one knew whence, and whom the people nicknamed Coll Dhu (Black Coll), because of his sullen bearing and solitary habits. His dwelling they called the Devil's Inn, because no tired traveller had ever been asked to rest under its roof, nor friend known to cross its threshold. No one bore him company in his retreat but a wizen-faced old man, who shunned the good-morrow of the trudging peasant when he made occasional excursions to the nearest village for provisions for himself and master, and who was as secret as a stone concerning all the antecedents of both.

For the first year of their residence in the country, there had been much speculation as to who they were, and what they did with themselves up there among the clouds and eagles. Some said that Coll Dhu was a scion of the old family from whose hands the surrounding lands had passed; and that, embittered by poverty and pride, he had come to bury himself in solitude, and brood over his misfortunes. Others hinted of crime, and flight from another country; others again whispered of those who were cursed from their birth, and could never smile, nor yet make friends with a fellow-creature till the day of their death. But when two years had passed, the wonder had somewhat died out, and Coll Dhu was little thought of, except when a herd looking for sheep crossed the track of a big dark man walking the mountains gun in hand, to whom he did not dare say "Lord save you!" or when a housewife rocking her cradle of a winter's night, crossed herself as a gust of storm thundered over her cabin-roof, with the exclamation, "Oh, then, it's Coll Dhu that has enough o' the fresh air about his head up there this night, the crature!"

Coll Dhu had lived thus in his solitude for some years, when it became known that Colonel Blake, the new lord of the soil, was coming to visit the country. By climbing one of the peaks encircling his eyrie, Coll could look sheer down a mountain-side, and see in miniature beneath him, a grey old dwelling with ivied chimneys and weather-slated walls, standing amongst straggling trees and grim warlike rocks, that gave it the look of a fortress, gazing out to the Atlantic for ever with the eager eyes of all its windows, as if demanding perpetually, "What tidings from the New World?"

He could see now masons and carpenters crawling about below, like ants in the sun, overrunning the old house from base to chimney, daubing here and knocking there, tumbling down walls that looked to Coll, up among the clouds, like a handful of jackstones, and building up others that looked like the toy fences in a child's Farm. Throughout several months he must have watched the busy ants at their task of breaking and mending again, disfiguring and beautifying; but when all was done he had not the curiosity to stride down and admire the handsome paneling of the new billiard-room, nor yet the fine view which the enlarged bay-window in the drawing-room commanded of the watery highway to Newfoundland.

Deep summer was melting into autumn, and the amber streaks of decay were beginning to creep out and trail over the ripe purple of moor and mountain, when Colonel Blake, his only daughter, and a party of friends, arrived in the country. The grey house below was alive with gaiety, but Coll Dhu no longer found an interest in observing it from his eyrie. When he watched the sun rise or set, he chose to ascend some crag that looked on no human habitation. When he sallied forth on his excursions, gun in hand, he set his face towards the most isolated wastes, dipping into the loneliest valleys, and scaling the nakedest ridges. When he came by chance within call of other excursionists, gun in hand he plunged into the shade of some hollow, and avoided an encounter. Yet it was fated, for all that, that he and Colonel Blake should meet.

Towards the evening of one bright September day, the wind changed, and in half an hour the mountains were wrapped in a thick blinding mist. Coll Dhu was far from his den, but so well had he searched these mountains, and inured himself to their climate, that neither storm, rain, nor fog, had power to disturb him. But while he stalked on his way, a faint and agonised cry from a human voice reached him through the smothering mist. He quickly tracked the sound, and gained the side of a man who was stumbling along in danger of death at every step.

"Follow me!" said Coll Dhu to this man, and, in an hour's time, brought him safely to the lowlands, and up to the walls of the eager-eyed mansion.

"I am Colonel Blake," said the frank soldier, when, having left the fog behind him, they stood in the starlight under the lighted windows. "Pray tell me quickly to whom I owe my life."

As he spoke, he glanced up at his benefactor, a large man with a sombre sun-burned face.

"Colonel Blake," said Coll Dhu, after a strange pause, "your father suggested to my father to stake his estates at the gaming table. They were staked, and the tempter won. Both are dead; but you and I live, and I have sworn to injure you."

The colonel laughed good humouredly at the uneasy face above him.

"And you began to keep your oath to-night by saving my life?" said he. "Come! I am a soldier, and know how to meet an enemy; but I had far rather meet a friend. I shall not be happy till you have eaten my salt. We have merry-making to-night in honour of my daughter's birthday. Come in and join us?"

Coll Dhu looked at the earth doggedly.

"I have told you," he said, "who and what I am, and I will not cross your threshold."

But at this moment (so runs my story) a French window opened among the flower-beds by which they were standing, and a vision appeared which stayed the words on Coll's tongue. A stately girl, clad in white satin, stood framed in the ivied window, with the warm light from within streaming around her richly-moulded figure into the night. Her face was as pale as her gown, her eyes were swimming in tears, but a firm smile sat on her lips as she held out both hands to her father. The light behind her, touched the glistening folds of her dress—the lustrous pearls round her throat—the coronet of blood-red roses which encircled the knotted braids at the back of her head. Satin, pearls, and roses—had Coll Dhu, of the Devil's Inn, never set eyes upon such things before?

Evleen Blake was no nervous tearful miss. A few quick words—"Thank God! you're safe; the rest have been home an hour"—and a tight pressure of her father's fingers between her own jewelled hands, were all that betrayed the uneasiness she had suffered.

"Faith, my love, I owe my life to this brave gentleman!" said the blithe colonel. "Press him to come in and be our guest, Evleen. He wants to retreat to his mountains, and lose himself again in the fog where I found him; or, rather, where he found me! Come, sir" (to Coll), "you must surrender to this fair besieger."

An introduction followed. "Coll Dhu!" murmured Evleen Blake, for she had heard the common tales of him; but with a frank welcome she invited her father's preserver to taste the hospitality of that father's house.

"I beg you to come in, sir," she said; "but

for you our gaiety must have been turned into mourning. A shadow will be upon our mirth if our benefactor disdains to join in it."

With a sweet grace, mingled with a certain hauteur from which she was never free, she extended her white hand to the tall looming figure outside the window; to have it grasped and wrung in a way that made the proud girl's eyes flash their amazement, and the same little hand clench itself in displeasure, when it had hid itself like an outraged thing among the shining folds of her gown. Was this Coll Dhu mad, or rude?

The guest no longer refused to enter, but followed the white figure into a little study where a lamp burned; and the gloomy stranger, the bluff colonel, and the young mistress of the house, were fully discovered to each other's eyes. Evleen glanced at the new comer's dark face, and shuddered with a feeling of indescribable dread and dislike; then, to her father, accounted for the shudder after a popular fashion, saying lightly: "There is some one walking over my grave."

So Coll Dhu was present at Evleen Blake's birthday ball. Here he was, under a roof which ought to have been his own, a stranger, known only by a nickname, shunned and solitary. Here he was, who had lived among the eagles and foxes, lying in wait with a fell purpose, to be revenged on the son of his father's foe for poverty and disgrace, for the broken heart of a dead mother, for the loss of a self-slaughtered father, for the dreary scattering of brothers and sisters. Here he stood, a Samson shorn of his strength; and all because a haughty girl had melting eyes, a winning mouth, and looked radiant in satin and roses.

Peerless where many were lovely, she moved among her friends, trying to be unconscious of the gloomy fire of those strange eyes which followed her unweariedly wherever she went. And when her father begged her to be gracious to the unsocial guest whom he would fain conciliate, she courteously conducted him to see the new picture-gallery adjoining the drawing-rooms; explained under what odd circumstances the colonel had picked up this little painting or that; using every delicate art her pride would allow to achieve her father's purpose, whilst maintaining at the same time her own personal reserve; trying to divert the guest's oppressive attention from herself to the objects for which she claimed his notice. Coll Dhu followed his conductress and listened to her voice, but what she said mattered nothing; nor did she wring many words of comment or reply from his lips, until they paused in a retired corner where the light was dim, before a window from which the curtain was withdrawn. The sashes were open, and nothing was visible but water; the night Atlantic, with the full moon riding high above a bank of clouds, making silvery tracks outward towards the distance of infinite mystery dividing two worlds. Here the following little scene is said to have been enacted.

"This window of my father's own planning,

is it not creditable to his taste?" said the young hostess, as she stood, herself glittering like a dream of beauty, looking on the moonlight.

Coll Dhu made no answer; but suddenly, it is said, asked her for a rose from a cluster of flowers that nestled in the lace on her bosom.

For the second time that night Evleen Blake's eyes flashed with no gentle light. But this man was the saviour of her father. She broke off a blossom, and with such good grace, and also with such queen-like dignity as she might assume, presented it to him. Whereupon, not only was the rose seized, but also the hand that gave it, which was hastily covered with kisses.

Then her anger burst upon him.

"Sir," she cried, "if you are a gentleman you must be mad! If you are not mad, then you are not a gentleman!"

"Be merciful," said Coll Dhu; "I love you. My God, I never loved a woman before! Ah!" he cried, as a look of disgust crept over her face, "you hate me. You shuddered the first time your eyes met mine. I love you, and you hate me!"

"I do," cried Evleen, vehemently, forgetting everything but her indignation. "Your presence is like something evil to me. Love me?—your looks poison me. Pray, sir, talk no more to me in this strain."

"I will trouble you no longer," said Coll Dhu. And, stalking to the window, he placed one powerful hand upon the sash, and vaulted from it out of her sight.

Bare-headed as he was, Coll Dhu strode off to the mountains, but not towards his own home. All the remaining dark hours of that night he is believed to have walked the labyrinths of the hills, until dawn began to scatter the clouds with a high wind. Fasting, and on foot from sunrise the morning before, he was then glad enough to see a cabin right in his way. Walking in, he asked for water to drink, and a corner where he might throw himself to rest.

There was a wake in the house, and the kitchen was full of people, all wearied out with the night's watch; old men were dozing over their pipes in the chimney-corner, and here and there a woman was fast asleep with her head on a neighbour's knee. All who were awake crossed themselves when Coll Dhu's figure darkened the door, because of his evil name; but an old man of the house invited him in, and offering him milk, and promising him a roasted potato by-and-by, conducted him to a small room off the kitchen, one end of which was strewed with heather, and where there were only two women sitting gossiping over a fire.

"A thraveller," said the old man, nodding his head at the women, who nodded back, as if to say "he has the traveller's right." And Coll Dhu flung himself on the heather, in the furthest corner of the narrow room.

The women suspended their talk for a while; but presently, guessing the intruder to be asleep, resumed it in voices above a whisper.

There was but a patch of window with the grey dawn behind it, but Coll could see the figures by the firelight over which they bent: an old woman sitting forward with her withered hands extended to the embers, and a girl reclining against the hearth wall, with her healthy face, bright eyes, and crimson draperies, glowing by turns in the flickering blaze.

"I do' know," said the girl, "but it's the quarest marriage iver I h'ard of. Sure it's not three weeks since he tould right an' left that he hated her like poison!"

"Whist, asthoreen!" said the colliagh, bending forward confidentially; "throth an' we all know that o' him. But what could he do, the cratnre! When she put the burragh-bos on him!"

"The *what*?" asked the girl.

"Then the burragh-bos machree-o? That's the spanchel o' death, avourneen; an' well she has him tethered to her now, bad luck to her!"

The old woman rocked herself and stifled the Irish cry breaking from her wrinkled lips by burying her face in her cloak.

"But what is it?" asked the girl, eagerly. "What's the burragh-bos, anyways, an' where did she get it?"

"Och, och! it's not fit for comin' over to young ears, but cuggir (whisper), acushla! It's a sthrip o' the skin o' a corpse, peeled from the crown o' the head to the heel, without crack or split, or the charrm's broke; an' that, rowled up, an' put on a sthring roun' the neck o' the wan that's cowld by the wan that wants to be loved. An' sure enough it puts the fire in their hearts, hot an' sthrong, afore twinty-four hours is gone."

The girl had started from her lazy attitude, and gazed at her companion with eyes dilated by horror.

"Marciful Saviour!" she cried. "Not a sowl on airth would bring the curse out o' heaven by sich a black doin'!"

"Aisy, Biddeen alanna! an' there's wan that does it, an' isn't the divil. Arrah, asthoreen, did ye niver hear tell o' Pexie na Pishrogie, that lives betune two hills o' Maam Turk?"

"I h'ard o' her," said the girl, breathlessly.

"Well, sorra bit lie, but it's hersel' that does it. She'll do it for money any day. Sure they hunted her from the graveyard o' Salruck, where she had the dead raised; an' glory be to God! they would ha' murthered her, only they missed her thracks, an' couldn't bring it home to her afther."

"Whist, a-wauher" (my mother), said the girl; "here's the thraveller gettin' up to set off on his road again! Och, then, it's the short rest he tuk, the sowl!"

It was enough for Coll, however. He had got up, and now went back to the kitchen, where the old man had caused a dish of potatoes to be roasted, and earnestly pressed his visitor to sit down and eat of them. This Coll did readily; having recruited his strength by a meal, he betook himself to the mountains again,

just as the rising sun was flashing among the waterfalls, and sending the night mists drifting down the glens. By sundown the same evening he was striding over the hills of Maam Turk, asking of herds his way to the cabin of one Pexie na Pishrogie.

In a hovel on a brown desolate heath, with scared-looking hills flying off into the distance on every side, he found Pexie: a yellow-faced hag, dressed in a dark-red blanket, with elf-locks of coarse black hair protruding from under an orange kerchief swathed round her wrinkled jaws. She was bending over a pot upon her fire, where herbs were simmering, and she looked up with an evil glance when Coll Dhu darkened her door.

"The burragh-bos is it her honour wants?" she asked, when he had made known his errand.

"Ay, ay; but the arighad, the arighad (money) for Pexie. The burragh-bos is ill to get."

"I will pay," said Coll Dhu, laying a sovereign on the bench before her.

The witch sprang upon it, and chuckling, bestowed on her visitor a glance which made even Coll Dhu shudder.

"Her honour is a fine king," she said, "an' her is fit to get the burragh-bos. Ha! ha! her sall get the burragh-bos from Pexie. But the arighad is not enough. More, more!"

She stretched out her claw-like hand, and Coll dropped another sovereign into it. Whereupon she fell into more horrible convulsions of delight.

"Hark ye!" cried Coll. "I have paid you well, but if your infernal charm does not work, I will have you hunted for a witch!"

"Work!" cried Pexie, rolling up her eyes. "If Pexie's charrm not work, then her honour come back an' carry these bits o' mountain away on her back. Ay, her will work. If the colleen hate her honour like the old diaoul hersel', still an' withal her will love her honour like her own white sowl afore the sun sets or rises. That, (with a furtive leer,) or the colleen dhas go wild mad afore wan hour."

"Hag!" returned Coll Dhu; "the last part is a hellish invention of your own. I heard nothing of madness. If you want more money, speak out, but play none of your hideous tricks on me."

The witch fixed her cunning eyes on him, and took her cue at once from his passion.

"Her honour guess thrue," she simpered; "it is only the little bit more arighad poor Pexie want."

Again the skinny hand was extended. Coll Dhu shrank from touching it, and threw his gold upon the table.

"King, king!" chuckled Pexie. "Her honour is a grand king. Her honour is fit to get the burragh-bos. The colleen dhas sall love her like her own white sowl. Ha, ha!"

"When shall I get it?" asked Coll Dhu, impatiently.

"Her honour sall come back to Pexie in so many days, do-deag (twelve), so many days, fur that the burragh-bos is hard to get. The lonely graveyard is far away, an' the dead man is hard to raise——"

"Silence!" cried Coll Dhu; "not a word more. I will have your hideous charm, but what it is, or where you get it, I will not know."

Then, promising to come back in twelve days, he took his departure. Turning to look back when a little way across the heath, he saw Pexie gazing after him, standing on her black hill in relief against the lurid flames of the dawn, seeming to his dark imagination like a fury with all hell at her back.

At the appointed time Coll Dhu got the promised charm. He sewed it with perfumes into a cover of cloth of gold, and slung it to a fine-wrought chain. Lying in a casket which had once held the jewels of Coll's broken-hearted mother, it looked a glittering bauble enough. Meantime the people of the mountains were cursing over their cabin fires, because there had been another unholy raid upon their graveyard, and were banding themselves to hunt the criminal down.

A fortnight passed. How or where could Coll Dhu find an opportunity to put the charm round the neck of the colonel's proud daughter? More gold was dropped into Pexie's greedy claw, and then she promised to assist him in his dilemma.

Next morning the witch dressed herself in decent garb, smoothed her elf-locks under a snowy cap, smoothed the evil wrinkles out of her face, and with a basket on her arm locked the door of the hovel, and took her way to the lowlands. Pexie seemed to have given up her disreputable calling for that of a simple mushroom-gatherer. The housekeeper at the grey house bought poor Muireade's mushrooms of her every morning. Every morning she left unfailingly a nosegay of wild flowers for Miss Evleen Blake, "God bless her! She had never seen the darling young lady with her own two longing eyes, but sure hadn't she heard tell of her sweet purty face, miles away!" And at last, one morning, whom should she meet but Miss Evleen herself returning alone from a ramble. Whereupon poor Muireade "made bold" to present her flowers in person.

"Ah," said Evleen, "it is you who leave me the flowers every morning? They are very sweet."

Muireade had sought her only for a look at her beautiful face. And now that she had seen it, as bright as the sun, and as fair as the lily, she would take up her basket and go away contented. Yet she lingered a little longer.

"My lady never walk up big mountain?" said Pexie.

"No," Evleen said, laughing; she feared she could not walk up a mountain.

"Ah yes; my lady ought to go, with more gran' ladies an' gentlemen, ridin' on purty little donkeys, up the big mountain. Oh, gran' things up big mountain for my lady to see!"

Thus she set to work, and kept her listener enchained for an hour, while she related wonderful stories of those upper regions. And as Evleen looked up to the burly crowns of the hills, perhaps she thought there might be sense in this wild old woman's suggestion. It ought to be a grand world up yonder.

Be that as it may, it was not long after this when Coll Dhu got notice that a party from the grey house would explore the mountains next day; that Evleen Blake would be of the number; and that he, Coll, must prepare to house and refresh a crowd of weary people, who in the evening should be brought, hungry and faint, to his door. The simple mushroom gatherer should be discovered laying in her humble stock among the green places between the hills, should volunteer to act as guide to the party, should lead them far out of their way through the mountains and up and down the most toilsome ascents and across dangerous places; to escape safely from which, the servants should be told to throw away the baskets of provisions which they carried.

Coll Dhu was not idle. Such a feast was set forth, as had never been spread so near the clouds before. We are told of wonderful dishes furnished by unwholesome agency, and from a place believed much hotter than is necessary for purposes of cookery. We are told also how Coll Dhu's barren chambers were suddenly hung with curtains of velvet, and with fringes of gold; how the blank white walls glowed with delicate colours and gilding; how gems of pictures sprang into sight between the panels; how the tables blazed with plate and gold, and glittered with the rarest glass; how such wines flowed, as the guests had never tasted; how servants in the richest livery, amongst whom the wizen-faced old man was a mere nonentity, appeared, and stood ready to carry in the wonderful dishes, at whose extraordinary fragrance the eagles came pecking to the windows, and the foxes drew near the walls, snuffing. Sure enough, in all good time, the weary party came within sight of the Devil's Inn, and Coll Dhu sallied forth to invite them across his lonely threshold. Colonel Blake (to whom Evleen, in her delicacy, had said no word of the solitary's strange behaviour to herself) hailed his appearance with delight, and the whole party sat down to Coll's banquet in high good humour. Also, it is said, in much amazement at the magnificence of the mountain recluse.

All went in to Coll's feast, save Evleen Blake, who remained standing on the threshold of the outer door; weary, but unwilling to rest there; hungry, but unwilling to eat there. Her white cambric dress was gathered on her arms, crushed and sullied with the toils of the day; her bright cheek was a little sun-burned; her small dark head with its braids a little tossed, was bared to the mountain air and the glory of the sinking sun; her hands were loosely tangled in the strings of her hat; and her foot sometimes tapped the threshold stone. So she was seen.

The peasants tell that Coll Dhu and her father came praying her to enter, and that the magnificent servants brought viands to the threshold; but no step would she move inward, no morsel would she taste.

"Poison, poison!" she murmured, and threw the food in handfuls to the foxes, who were snuffing on the heath.

But it was different when Muireade, the kindly old woman, the simple mushroom-gatherer, with all the wicked wrinkles smoothed out of her face, came to the side of the hungry girl, and coaxingly presented a savoury mess of her own sweet mushrooms, served on a common earthen platter.

"An' darlin', my lady, poor Muireade her cook them hersel', an' no thing o' this house touch them or look at poor Muireade's mushrooms."

Then Evleen took the platter and ate a delicious meal. Scarcely was it finished when a heavy drowsiness fell upon her, and, unable to sustain herself on her feet, she presently sat down upon the door-stone. Leaning her head against the framework of the door, she was soon in a deep sleep, or trance. So she was found.

"Whimsical, obstinate little girl!" said the colonel, putting his hand on the beautiful slumbering head. And taking her in his arms, he carried her into a chamber which had been (say the story-tellers) nothing but a bare and sorry closet in the morning, but which was now fitted up with Oriental splendour. And here on a luxurious couch she was laid, with a crimson coverlet wrapping her feet. And here in the tempered light coming through jewelled glass, where yesterday had been a coarse rough-hung window, her father looked his last upon her lovely face.

The colonel returned to his host and friends, and by-and-by the whole party sallied forth to see the after-glare of a fierce sunset swathing the hills in flames. It was not until they had gone some distance that Coll Dhu remembered to go back and fetch his telescope. He was not long absent. But he was absent long enough to enter that glowing chamber with a stealthy step, to throw a light chain around the neck of the sleeping girl, and to slip among the folds of her dress the hideous glittering burragh-bos.

After he had gone away again, Pexie came stealing to the door, and, opening it a little, sat down on the mat outside, with her cloak wrapped round her. An hour passed, and Evleen Blake still slept, her breathing scarcely stirring the deadly bauble on her breast. After that, she began to murmur and moan, and Pexie pricked up her ears. Presently a sound in the room told that the victim was awake and had risen. Then Pexie put her face to the aperture of the door and looked in, gave a howl of dismay, and fled from the house, to be seen in that country no more.

The light was fading among the hills, and the ramblers were returning towards the Devil's Inn, when a group of ladies who were considerably in advance of the rest, met Evleen Blake advancing towards them on the heath, with her hair disordered as by sleep, and no covering on her head. They noticed something bright, like gold, shifting and glancing with the motion of her figure. There had been some jesting among them about Evleen's fancy for falling asleep on the door-step instead of coming in to dinner, and they advanced laughing, to rally her on the subject. But she stared at them in a strange way, as if she did not know them, and passed on. Her friends were rather offended, and commented on her fantastic humour; only one looked after her, and got laughed at by her companions for expressing uneasiness on the wilful young lady's account.

So they kept their way, and the solitary figure went fluttering on, the white robe blushing, and the fatal burragh-bos glittering in the reflexion from the sky. A hare crossed her path, and she laughed out loudly, and clapping her hands, sprang after it. Then she stopped and asked questions of the stones, striking them with her open palm because they would not answer. (An amazed little herd sitting behind a rock, witnessed these strange proceedings.) By-and-by she began to call after the birds, in a wild shrill way, startling the echoes of the hills as she went along. A party of gentlemen returning by a dangerous path, heard the unusual sound and stopped to listen.

"What is that?" asked one.

"A young eagle," said Coll Dhu, whose face had become livid; "they often give such cries."

"It was uncommonly like a woman's voice!" was the reply; and immediately another wild note rang towards them from the rocks above: a bare saw-like ridge, shelving away to some distance ahead, and projecting one hungry tooth over an abyss. A few more moments and they saw Evleen Blake's light figure fluttering out towards this dizzy point.

"My Evleen!" cried the colonel, recognising his daughter, "she is mad to venture on such a spot!"

"Mad!" repeated Coll Dhu. And then dashed off to the rescue with all the might and swiftness of his powerful limbs.

When he drew near her, Evleen had almost reached the verge of the terrible rock. Very cautiously he approached her, his object being to seize her in his strong arms before she was aware of his presence, and carry her many yards away from the spot of danger. But in a fatal moment Evleen turned her head and saw him. One wild ringing cry of hate and horror, which startled the very eagles and scattered a flight of curlews above her head, broke from her lips. A step backward brought her within a foot of death.

One desperate though wary stride, and she was struggling in Coll's embrace. One glance in her eyes, and he saw that he was striving with a mad woman. Back, back, she dragged him, and he had nothing to grasp by. The rock was slippery and his shod feet would not cling to it. Back, back! A hoarse panting, a dire swinging to and fro; and then the rock was

standing naked against the sky, no one was
there, and Coll Dhu and Evleen Blake lay
shattered far below.

III.

TO BE TAKEN AT THE DINNER-TABLE.

Does any one know who gives the names to
our streets? Does any one know who invents
the mottoes which are inserted in the cracker-
papers, along with the sugar-plums?—I don't
envy him his intellectual faculties, by-the-by, and
I suspect him to be the individual who trans-
lates the books of the foreign operas. Does any
one know who introduces the new dishes,
Kromeski's, and such-like? Does any one know
who is responsible for new words, such as shunt
and thud, shimmer, ping (denoting the crack of
the rifle), and many others? Does any one
know who has obliged us to talk for ever about
"fraternising" and "cropping up"? Does any
one know the Sage to whom perfumers apply
when they have invented a shaving-soap, or hair-
wash, and who furnishes the trade with such
names for their wares as Rypophagon, Euxesis,
Depilatory, Bostrakeison? Does any one know
who makes the riddles?

To the last question—only—I answer, Yes ;
I know.

In a certain year, which, I don't mind mentioning may be looked upon as included in
the present century, I was a little boy—a sharp
little boy, though I say it, and a skinny little
boy. The two qualities not unfrequently go together. I will not mention what my age was at
the time, but I was at school not far from
London, and I was of an age when it is customary, or *was* customary, to wear a jacket and
frill.

In riddles, I had at that early age a profound
and solemn joy. To the study of those problems,
I was beyond measure addicted, and in the col-
lecting of them I was diligent in the extreme.
It was the custom at the time for certain periodicals to give the question of a conundrum in one
number, and the answer in the next. There
was an interval of seven days and nights
between the propounding of the question, and
the furnishing of the reply. What a time was
that for me! I sought the solution of the
enigma, off and on (generally on), during the
leisure hours of the week (no wonder I was
skinny!), and sometimes, I am proud to remember, I became acquainted with the answer before
the number containing it reached me from the
official source. There was another kind of
puzzle which used to appear when my sharp
and skinny boyhood was at its sharpest and
skinniest, by which I was much more perplexed
than by conundrums or riddles conveyed in
mere words. I speak of what may be called
symbolical riddles—rebus is, I believe, their
true designation—little squalid woodcuts repre-
senting all sorts of impossible objects huddled

together in incongruous disorder ; letters of the
alphabet, at times, and even occasionally frag-
ments of words, being introduced here and there,
to add to the general confusion. Thus you would
have : a Cupid mending a pen, a gridiron, the
letter x, a bar of music, p. u. g. and a fife—
you would have these presented to you on a
certain Saturday, with the announcement that
on the following Saturday there would be is-
sued an explanation of the mysterious and terrific
jumble. That explanation would come, but with
it new difficulties worse than the former. A
birdcage, a setting sun (not like), the word
"snip," a cradle, and some quadruped to which
it would have puzzled Buffon himself to give a
name. With these problems I was not success-
ful, never having solved but one in my life, as
will presently appear. Neither was I good at
poetical riddles, in parts—slightly forced—as
"My first is a boa-constrictor, My second's a
Roman lictor, My third is a Dean and Chipter,
And my whole goes always on tip-ter." These
were too much for me.

I remember on one occasion accidentally
meeting with a publication in which there was
a rebus better executed than those to which I
had been accustomed, and which mystified me
greatly. First of all there was the letter A;
then came a figure of a clearly virtuous man
in a long gown, with a scrip, and a staff, and
a cockle-shell on his hat; then followed a re-
presentation of an extremely old person with
flowing white hair and beard; the figure 2
was the next symbol, and beyond this was a
gentleman on crutches, looking at a five-barred
gate. Oh, how that rebus haunted me! It was
at a sea-side library that I met with it during
the holidays, and before the next number came
out I was back at school. The publication in
which this remarkable picture had appeared was
an expensive one, and quite beyond my means,
so there was no way of getting at the explanation. Determined to conquer, and fearing that
one of the symbols might escape my memory,
I wrote them down in order. In doing so, an
interpretation flashed upon me. A—Pilgrim
—Age—To—Cripple—Gate. Ah! was it the
right one? Had I triumphed, or had I failed?
My anxiety on the subject attained such a
pitch at last, that I determined to write to the
editor of the periodical in which the rebus had
appeared, and implore him to take compassion
upon me and relieve my mind. To that communication I received no answer. Perhaps there
was one in the notices to correspondents—but
then I must have purchased the periodical to
get it.

I mention these particulars because they had
something—not a little—to do with a certain
small incident which, small though it was, had
influence on my after life. The incident in
question was the composition of a riddle by the
present writer. It was composed with difficulty,
on a slate ; portions of it were frequently rubbed
out, the wording of it gave me a world of
trouble, but the work was achieved at last.
"Why," it was thus that I worded it in its

final and corrected form, "Why does a young gentleman who has partaken freely of the pudding, which at this establishment precedes the meat, resemble a meteor?—Because he's effulgent—a full gent!"

Hopeful, surely! Nothing unnaturally premature in the composition. Founded on a strictly boyish grievance. Possessing a certain archæological interest in its reference to the now obsolete practice of administering pudding before meat at educational establishments, with the view of damping the appetite (and constitution) of the pupils.

Though inscribed upon perishable and greasy slate, in ephemeral slate-pencil, my riddle lived. It was repeated. It became popular. It was all over the school, and at last it came to the ears of the master. That unimaginative person had no taste for the fine arts. I was sent for, interrogated as to whether this work of art was the product of my brain, and, having given an answer in the affirmative, received a distinct, and even painful, punch on the head, accompanied by specific directions to inscribe straightway the words "Dangerous Satirising," two thousand times, on the very slate on which my riddle had been originally composed.

Notwithstanding this act of despotism on the part of the unappreciative Beast who invariably treated me as if I were not profitable (when I knew the contrary), my reverence for the great geniuses who have excelled in the department of which I am speaking, grew with my growth, and strengthened with &c. Think of the pleasure, the rapture, which Riddles afford to persons of wholesomely constituted mind! Think of the innocent sense of triumph felt by the man who propounds a riddle to a company, to every member of which it is a novelty. He alone is the proprietor of the answer. His is a glorious position. He keeps everybody waiting. He wears a calm and placid smile. He has the rest at his mercy. He is happy——innocently happy.

But who makes the Riddles?

I do.

Am I going to let out a great mystery? Am I going to initiate the uninitiated? Am I going to let the world know *how it is done?* Yes. I am.

It is done in the main by the Dictionary; but the consultation of that work of reference, with a view to the construction of riddles, is a process so bewildering—it puts such a strain upon the faculties—that at first you cannot work at it for more than a quarter of an hour at once. The process is terrific. First of all you get yourself thoroughly awake and on the alert—it is good to run the fingers through the hair roughly at this crisis—then you take your Dictionary, and, selecting a particular letter, you go down the column, stopping at every word that looks in the slightest degree promising, drawing back from it as artists draw back from a picture to see it the better, twisting it, and turning it, and if it yield nothing, passing on to the next. With the substantives you occupy yourself in an

especial manner, as more may be done with them than with any of the other parts of speech; while as to the words with two meanings, you must be in a bad state indeed, or have particularly ill luck, if you fail to get something out of them.

Suppose that you are going in' for a day's riddling—your dinner depending on the success of your efforts. I take your Dictionary, and open it at hap-hazard. You open, say, among the Fs, and you go to work.

You make several stoppages as you go down the column. You pause naturally at the word Felt. It is a past participle of the verb to feel, and it is a substance used in making hats. You press it hard. Why is a hatter—No—Why may a hatter invariably be looked upon as a considerate person? Because he has always *felt* for—No. That won't do. You go on. "Fen"—a chance here for a well-timed thing about the Fenian Brotherhood. This is worth a struggle, and you make a desperate one. A Fen is a marsh. In a marsh there is mud. Why was it always to be expected that the Irish rebels must ultimately stick in the mud? Because theirs was a *Fen*-ian movement.—Intolerable! Yet you are loth to abandon the subject. A Fen is a Morass. More-ass. Why is an Irish rebel more ass than knave? No, again it won't do!

Disconsolate, but dogged, you go on till you arrive at "Fertile." Fer-tile. Tile—Tile, a Hat. Why is a Hat made of Beaver, like land that always yields fine crops? Because it may be called Fertile (Fur-tile). That will do. Not first-class, but it will do. Riddling is very like fishing. Sometimes you get a small trout, sometimes a large one. This is a small trout, but it shall go into the basket, nevertheless. And now you are fairly warming to your work. You come to "Forgery." You again make a point. Forgery. For-gery — For Jerry. A complicated riddle of a high order. Intricate, and of the Coleridge kind. Why—No, If—If a gentleman, having a favourite son of tender years, named Jeremiah, were in the course of dessert to put a pear in his pocket, stating, as he did so, that the fruit was intended for his beloved boy, why, in making such an explanation, would he mention a certain act of felony once punishable by death? — Because he would say that it was Forgery—For Jerry. Into the basket.

It never rains but it pours. Another complex one, of the same type. Fungus! If a well-bred lady should, in sport, poke her cousin *Augustus* in the ribs with her lilac and white parasol, and hurt him, what vegetable product would she mention in facetiously apologising? Fungus. Fun Gus! In with it.

The Fs being exhausted, you take a short rest. Then, screwing your faculties up afresh, and seizing the Dictionary again, you open it once more. Cs this time lie before you, a page of Cs. You pause, hopeful, at corn. The word has two meanings, it ought to answer. It shall be made to answer. This is a case of a peculiar kind. You determine to construct a riddle by rule. There is no genius needed here. The word has two meanings; both shall be used; it is a mechanical process. Why is a reaper at his work, like a chiropodist?—Because he's a corn-cutter. Made by rule, complete, impregnable; but yet not interesting. The Cs are not propitious, and you apply to the Bs. In your loitering mood you drop down upon the word "Bring," and with idiotcy at hand sit gazing at it. Suddenly you revive—Bring, Brought, Brought up. Brought up will do. Why is the coal-scuttle which Mary has conveyed from the kitchen to the second floor, like an infant put out to dry-nurse?—Because it's brought up by hand. You try once more, and this time it is the letter H on which your hopes depend. The columns under H, duly perused, bring you in due time to Horse. Why is a horse attached to the vehicle of a miser, like a war-steamer of the present day?—Because he's driven by a screw. Another? Hoarse. Why is a family, the members of which have always been subject to sore-throats, like "The Derby?"—Because it's a hoarse-race (Horse-race).

It is by no means always the case, however, that the Dictionary affords so large a yield as this. It is hard work—exhausting work—and, worst of all, *there is no end to it.* You get, after a certain time, incapable of shaking off the shop even in your moments of relaxation. Nay, worse. You feel as if you *ought* to be always at it, lest you should miss a good chance, that would never return. It is this that makes epigrammatic literature wearing. If you go to the play, if you take up a newspaper, if you ensconce yourself in a corner with a blessed work of fiction, you find yourself still pursued and haunted by your profession. The dialogue to which you listen when you go to the theatre, the words of the book you are reading, may suggest something, and it behoves you to be on the look-out. Horrible and distracting calling! You may get rid of your superfluous flesh more quickly by going through a course of riddling, than by running up-hill in blankets for a week together, or going through a systematic course of Turkish baths.

Moreover, the cultivator of epigrammatic literature has much to undergo in the disposal of his wares, when they are once ready for the market. There is a public sale for them, and, between ourselves, there is a private ditto. The public demand for the article, which it has been so long my lot to supply, is not large, nor, I am constrained to say, is it entirely cordial. The periodicals in which your rebus or your conundrum appears hebdomadally, are not numerous; nor are the proprietors of such journals respectfully eager for this peculiar kind of literature. The conundrum or the rebus will knock about the office for a long time, and, perhaps, only get inserted at last because it fits a vacant space. When we *are* inserted, we always —always mind—occupy an ignoble place. We come in at the bottom of a column, or occupy the very last lines of the periodical in which we appear—in company with that inevitable game

at chess in which white is to check-mate in four moves. One of the best riddles—*the* best, I think, that I ever made—was knocking about at the office of a certain journal six weeks before it got before the public. It ran thus: Why is a little man who is always telling long stories about nothing, like a certain new kind of rifle? ANSWER: Because he's a small-bore.

This work was the means of bringing me acquainted with the fact that there was a Private as well as a Public sale for the productions of the epigrammatic artist. A gentleman, who did not give his name—neither will I give it, though I know it well—called at the office of the periodical in which this particular riddle appeared, on the day succeeding its publication, and asked for the name and address of its author. The sub-editor of the journal, a fast friend of mine, to whom I owe many a good turn, furnished him with both, and, on a certain day, a middle-aged gentleman of rather plethoric appearance, with a sly twinkle in his eye, and with humorous lines about his mouth—both eye and mouth were utter impostors, for my friend had not a particle of humour in his composition—came gasping up my stairs, and introducing himself as an admirer of genius—"and therefore," he added, with a courteous wave of the hand, "your very humble servant"—wished to know whether it would suit my purpose to supply him, from time to time, with certain specimens of epigrammatic literature, now a riddle, now an epigram, now a short story that could be briefly and effectively told, all of which should be guaranteed to be entirely new and original, which should be made over wholly and solely to him, and to which no other human being should have access on any consideration whatever. My gentleman added that he was prepared to pay very handsomely for what he had, and, indeed, mentioned terms which caused me to open my eyes to the fullest extent of which those organs are capable.

I soon found out what my friend Mr. Price Scrooper was at. I call him by this name (which is fictitious, but something like his own), for the sake of convenience. He was a diner-out, who held a somewhat precarious reputation, which, by hook or crook, he had acquired as a sayer of good things, a man sure to have the last new story at the end of his tongue. Mr. Scrooper liked dining-out above all things, and the horror of that day when there should come a decline in the number of his invitations was always before his eyes. Thus it came about that relations were established between us—between me, the epigrammatic artist, and Price Scrooper, the diner-out.

I fitted him with a good thing or two even on the very day of his paying me a first visit. I gave him a story which I remembered to have heard my father tell when I was an infant—a perfectly safe story, which had been buried for years in oblivion. I supplied him with a riddle or two which I happened to have by me, and which were so very bad that no company could ever suspect them of a professional origin. I set him up in epigram for some time, and he set me up in the necessaries of life for some time, and so we parted mutually satisfied.

The commercial dealings thus satisfactorily established were renewed steadily and at frequent intervals. Of course, as in all earthly relations, there were not wanting some unpleasant elements to qualify the generally comfortable arrangements. Mr. Scrooper would sometimes complain that some of the witticisms with which I had supplied him, had failed in creating an effect—had hardly proved remunerative, in short. What could I reply? I could not tell him that this was his fault. I told him a story given by Isaac Walton, of a clergyman who, hearing a sermon preached by one of his cloth with immense effect, asked for the loan of it. On returning the sermon, however, after having tried it on his own congregation, he complained that it had proved a total failure, and that his audience had responded in no degree to his eloquence. The answer of the original proprietor of the sermon was crushing: "I lent you," he said, "indeed, my fiddle, but not my fiddle-stick;" meaning, as Isaac explains, rather unnecessarily, "the manner and intelligence with which the sermon was to be delivered."

My friend did not seem to feel the application of this anecdote. I believe he was occupied, while I spoke, in committing the story to his memory for future use—thus getting it gratuitously out of me—which was mean.

In fact, Mr. Scrooper, besides his original irreparable deficiency, was getting old and stupid, and would often forget or misapply the point of a story, or the answer to a conundrum. With these last I supplied him freely, working really hard to prepare for his use such articles as were adapted to his peculiar exigencies. As a diner-out, riddles of a convivial sort—alluding to matters connected with the pleasures of the table—are generally in request, and with a supply of these I fitted Mr. Scrooper, much to his satisfaction. Here are some specimens, for which I charged him rather heavily:

Why is wine—observe how easily this is brought in after dinner—why is wine, made up for the British market, like a deserter from the army?

Because it's always brandied (branded) before it's sent off.

Why is a ship, which has to encounter rough weather before it reaches its destination, like a certain wine which is usually adulterated with logwood and other similar matters?

Because it goes through a vast deal before it comes into port.

What portion of the trimming of a lady's dress resembles East India sherry of the first quality?

That which goes round the Cape.

One of his greatest difficulties, my patron told me—for he was as frank with me as a man is with his doctor or his lawyer—was in remembering which were the houses where he had related a certain story, or propounded a certain conun-

drum; who were the people to whom such and such a riddle would be fresh; who were the people to whom it was already but too familiar. Mr. Scrooper had also a habit of sometimes asking the answer to a riddle instead of the question, which was occasionally productive of confusion; or, giving the question properly, he would, when his audience became desperate and gave it up, supply them with the answer to an altogether different conundrum.

One day, my patron came to me in a state of high indignation. A riddle—bran new, and for which I had demanded a high price, thinking well of it myself—had failed, and Mr. Scrooper came to me in a rage to expostulate.

"It fell as flat as ditch-water," he said. "Indeed, one very disagreeable person said there was nothing in it, and he thought there must be some mistake. A very nasty thing to say, considering that the riddle was given as my own. How could I be mistaken in my own riddle?"

"May I ask," said I, politely, "how you worded the question?"

"Certainly. I worded it thus: Why are we justified in believing that the pilgrims to Mecca, undertake the journey with mercenary motives?"

"Quite right," said I; "and the answer?"

"The answer," replied my patron, "was as you gave it me: Because they go for the sake of Mahomet."

"I am not surprised," I said, coldly, for I felt that I had been unjustly blamed, "that your audience was mystified. The answer, as I gave it to you, ran thus: Because they go for the sake of the profit (Prophet)!"

Mr. Scrooper subsequently apologised.

I draw near to the end of my narrative. The termination is painful, so is that of King Lear. The worst feature in it is, that it involves the acknowledgment of a certain deplorable piece of weakness on my own part.

I was really in the receipt of a very pretty little income from Mr. Scrooper, when one morning I was again surprised by a visit from a total stranger—again, as on a former occasion, a middle-aged gentleman—again an individual with a twinkling eye and a humorous mouth —again a diner-out, with two surnames—Mr. Kerby Postlethwaite I will call him, which is sailing as near the wind as I consider safe.

Mr. Kerby Postlethwaite came on the errand which had already brought Mr. Scrooper to the top of my stairs. He, too, had seen one of my productions in a certain journal (for I still kept up my relation with the public press), and he too having a similar reputation to maintain, and finding his brain at times rather sterile, had come to me to make exactly the same proposal which had already been made by Mr. Price Scrooper.

For a time the singularity of the coincidence absolutely took my breath away, and I remained staring speechlessly at my visitor in a manner which might have suggested to him that I was hardly the man to furnish him with anything very brilliant. However, I managed to recover myself in time. I was very guarded and careful in my speech, but finally expressed my readiness to come to terms with my new employer. These were soon settled: Mr. Kerby Postlethwaite having even more liberal views as to this part of the business than those entertained by Mr. Price Scrooper.

The only difficulty was to supply this gentleman quickly enough with what he wanted. He was in a hurry. He was going that very evening to a dinner-party, and it was supremely important that he should distinguish himself. The occasion was a special one. It must be something good. He would not stick at a trifle in the matter of terms, but he did want something super-excellent. A riddle—a perfectly new riddle—he would like best.

My stores were turned over, my desk was ransacked, and still he was not satisfied. Suddenly it flashed into my mind that I had something by me which would exactly do. The very thing; a riddle alluding to a subject of the day; a subject just at that time in everybody's mouth. One which there would be no difficulty in leading up to. In short, a very neat thing indeed. There was but one doubt in my mind. Had I already sold it to my original employer? That was the question, and for the life of me I could not answer it with certainty. The life of one addicted to such pursuits as mine, is chaotic; and with me more particularly, doing an extensive public and private trade, it was especially so. I kept no books, nor any record of my professional transactions. One thing which influenced me strongly to believe the riddle to be still unappropriated, was, that I had certainly received no intelligence as to its success or failure from Mr. Scrooper, whereas that gentleman never failed to keep me informed on that momentous point. I was in doubt, but I ended (so princely were the terms offered by my new patron) in giving myself the benefit of that doubt, and handing over the work of art in question to Mr. Kerby Postlethwaite.

If I were to say that I felt comfortable after having brought this transaction to a close, I should not speak the truth. Horrible misgivings filled my mind, and there were moments when, if it had been possible to undo what was done, I should have taken that retrogressive step. This, however, was out of the question. I didn't even know where my new employer was to be found. I had nothing for it but to wait and try my best to feel sanguine.

The circumstances which distinguished the evening of that eventful day on which I first received a visit from my new patron, were subsequently related to me with great accuracy, and not without rancorous comment, by both of those who sustained leading parts in the evening's performances. Yes, terrible to relate, on the following day both my patrons came to me, overflowing with fury, to tell me what had happened, and to denounce me as the first cause of the mischief. Both were furious, but my more recent acquaintance, Mr. Postlethwaite, was the more vehement in his wrath.

It appeared, according to this gentleman's statement, that having repaired at the proper time to the residence of the gentleman whose guest he was to be that evening, and who, he took occasion to inform me, was a personage of consideration, he found himself in the midst of a highly distinguished company. He had intended to be the last arrival, but a fellow named Scrooper, or Price, or something of that sort—both names, perhaps—was yet expected. He soon arrived, however, Mr. Postlethwaite said, and the company went down to dinner.

Throughout the meal, the magnificent nature of which I will not dilate upon, these two gentlemen were continually at loggerheads. They appear—and in this both the accounts which reached me tally—to have contradicted each other, interrupted each other, cut into each other's stories, on every occasion, until that sort of hatred was engendered between them which Christian gentlemen sharing a meal together do sometimes feel towards each other. I suspect that each had heard of the other as a "diner-out," though they had not met before, and that each was prepared to hate the other.

Adhering to the Postlethwaitean narrative faithfully, I find that all this time, and even when most aggravated by the conduct of my earliest patron, he was able to comfort himself with the reflection that he had by him in store the weapon wherewith, when the proper moment should arrive, to inflict the coup de grace upon his rival. That weapon was my riddle—my riddle fitted to a topic of the day.

The moment arrived. I shudder as I proceed. The meal was over, the wines had circulated once, and Mr. Kerby Postlethwaite began gently insidiously and with all the dexterity of an old performer, to lead the conversation in the direction of THE TOPIC. His place was very near to the seat occupied by my original patron, Mr. Price Scrooper. What was Mr. Postlethwaite's astonishment to hear that gentleman leading such conversation, as was within his jurisdiction, *also* in the direction of THE TOPIC! "Does he see that I want a lead, and is he playing into my hands?" thought my newest client. "Perhaps he's not such a bad fellow, after all. I'll do as much for him another time." This amicable view of the matter was but of brief duration. Madness was at hand! Two voices were presently heard speaking simultaneously:

MR. PRICE SCROOPER. The subject suggested a riddle to me this morning, as I was thinking it over.	Both speaking at once.
MR. KERBY POSTLETHWAITE. A view of the thing struck me in the light of a riddle, this morning, quite suddenly.	

The two were silent, each having stopped the other.

"I beg your pardon," said my first patron, with ferocious politeness, "you were saying that you——"

"Had made a riddle," replied my second

patron. "Yes. I think that you also alluded to your having done something of the sort?"

"I did."

There was silence all round the table. Some illustrious person broke it at last by saying, "What a strange coincidence!"

"At all events," cried the master of the house, "let us hear one of them. Come, Scrooper, you spoke first."

"Mr. Postlethwaite, I insist upon having your riddle," said the lady of the house, with whom Mr. P. was the favourite.

Under these circumstances both gentlemen paused, and then, each bursting forth suddenly, there was a renewal of duet.

> MR. PRICE SCROOPER. Why does the Atlantic cable, in its present condition— } Both speaking at once.
> MR. KERBY POSTLETHWAITE. Why does the Atlantic cable, in its present condition—

At this there was a general roar and commotion among those present. "Our riddles appear to be somewhat alike?" remarked Mr. Postlethwaite, in a bitter tone, and looking darkly at my first patron.

"It is the most extraordinary thing," replied that gentleman, "that I ever heard of!"

"Great wits jump," said the illustrious person who had previously spoken of an "extraordinary coincidence."

"At any rate, let us hear one of them," cried the host. "Perhaps they vary after the first few words. Come, Scrooper."

"Yes, let us hear one of them to the end," said the lady of the house, and she looked at Mr. Postlethwaite. This last, however, was sulky. Mr. Price Scrooper took advantage of the circumstance to come out with the conundrum in all its integrity.

"Why," asked this gentleman once more, "is the Atlantic cable, in its present condition, like a schoolmaster?"

"That is my riddle," said Mr. Postlethwaite, as soon as the other had ceased to speak. "I made it myself."

"On the contrary, it is mine, I assure you," replied Mr. Scrooper, very doggedly. "I composed it while shaving this morning."

Here again there was a pause, broken only by interjectional expressions of astonishment on the part of those who were present—led by the illustrious man.

Again the master of the house came to the rescue. "The best way of settling it," he said, "will be to ascertain which of our two friends knows the answer. Whoever knows the answer can claim the riddle. Let each of these gentlemen write down the answer on a piece of paper, fold it up, and give it to me. If the answers are identical, the coincidence will indeed be extraordinary."

"It is impossible that any one but myself can know the answer," remarked my first patron, as he wrote on his paper and folded it.

My second patron wrote also, and folded. "The answer," he said, "can only be known to me."

The papers were unfolded by the master of the house, and read one after the other.

ANSWER written by Mr. Price Scrooper: "Because it's supported by buoys (boys)."

ANSWER written by Mr. Kerby Postlethwaite: "Because it's supported by buoys (boys)."

There was a scene. There were recriminations. As I have said, on the following morning both gentlemen visited me betimes. They had not much to say after all. Were they not both in my power?

The curious thing is, that from that time dates the decline of my professional eminence. Of course, both my patrons took leave of me for ever. But I have also to relate that my powers of riddling took leave of me also. My mornings with the Dictionary became less and less productive of results, and, only a fortnight ago last Wednesday, I sent to a certain weekly publication a rebus presenting the following combination of objects: A giraffe, a haystack, a boy driving a hoop, the letter X, a crescent, a human mouth, the words "I wish," a dog standing on its hind legs, and a pair of scales. It appeared. It took. It puzzled the public. But for the life of me I cannot form the remotest idea what it meant, and I am ruined.

IV.

NOT TO BE TAKEN FOR GRANTED.

To-day I, Eunice Fielding, have been looking over the journal which I kept of the first few weeks of my life in the world, after I left the seclusion of the German Moravian school, where I was educated. I feel a strange pity for myself, the tender ignorant innocent school-girl, freed from the peaceful shelter of the Moravian settlement, and thrust suddenly into the centre of a sorrowful household.

As I turn to this first page, there rises before me, like the memory of a former life, a picture of the noiseless grass-grown streets of the settlement, with the old-fashioned dwellings, and the quiet and serene faces looking out kindly upon the troop of children passing to the church. There is the home of the Single Sisters, with its shining and spotless casements; and close beside it, is the church where they and we worshipped, with its broad central aisle always separating the women from the men. I can see the girls in their picturesque caps, trimmed with scarlet, and the blue ribbons of the matrons, and the pure white head-gear of the widows; the burial-ground, where the separation is still maintained, and where the brethren and the sisters lie in undivided graves; and the kindly simple-hearted pastor, who was always touched with the feeling of our weakness. I see it all, as I turn over the pages of my short journal, with just a faint longing to return to the repose and innocent ignorance which encircled me while I dwelt among them, safely shut in from the sorrows of the world.

Nov. 7. At home once more after an absence of three years; but home is changed. There used to be a feeling of mother's presence everywhere about the house, even if she were in the remotest room; but now, Susannah and Priscilla are wearing her apparel, and as they go in and out, and I catch a glimpse of the soft dove-coloured folds of the dresses, I look up with a start, half in hope of seeing my mother's face again. They are much older than I am, for Priscilla was ten years of age when I was born, and Susannah is three years older than Priscilla. They are very grave and serious, and it is well known, even in Germany, how religious they are. I suppose by the time I am as old as they are, I shall be the same.

I wonder if my father ever felt like a child; he looks as if he had lived for centuries. Last night I could not venture to look too closely into his face; but to-day I can see a very kind and peaceful expression underlying all the wrinkles and lines of care. In his soul there is a calm serene depth which no tempest can touch. That is plain. He is a good man, I know, though his goodness was not talked about at school, as was Susannah's and Priscilla's. When the coach set me down at the door, and he ran out into the street bareheaded, and took me at once into his arms, carrying me like a little child into our home, all my sorrow upon leaving my schoolfellows, and the sisters, and our pastor, passed away in the joy of being with him. God helping me—and surely he will help me to do this—I will be a comfort to my father.

The house is very different to what it was in my mother's time. The rooms look gloomy, for the walls are damp and mildewed, and the carpets are worn threadbare. It seems as if my sister had taken no pride in household matters. To be sure Priscilla is betrothed to one of the brethren, who dwells in Woodbury, about ten miles from here. She told me last night what a beautiful house he had, and how it was furnished with more luxury and costliness than our people often care for, inasmuch as we do not seek worldly show. She also displayed the fine linen she has been preparing for herself, with store of dresses, both in silks and stuffs. They looked so grand, spread out upon the poor furniture of our chamber, that I could not help but cast up in my own mind what the cost would be, and I inquired how my father's business prospered: at which Priscilla coloured, but Susannah uttered a low deep groan, which was answer enough.

This morning I unpacked my trunk, and gave a letter from the church to each of my sisters. It was to make known to them that Brother Schmidt, a missionary in the West Indies, desires that a fitting wife should be chosen for him by casting of lots, and sent out to him. Several of the single sisters in our settlement have given in their names, and such is the repute of Susannah and Priscilla, that they are notified of the application, that they may do likewise. Of course Priscilla, being already betrothed, has no thought of doing so; but Susannah has been deep in meditation all day, and now she is sitting opposite to me, pale and solemn, her brown hair, in which I can detect a silver thread or two, braided closely down her thin cheeks; but as she writes, a faint blush steals over her face, as if she were listening to Brother Schmidt, whom she has never seen, and whose voice she never heard. She has written her name—I can read it, "Susannah Fielding"—in her clear round steady hand, and it will be put into the lot with many others, from among which one will be drawn out, and the name written thereon will be that of Brother Schmidt's appointed wife.

Nov. 9. Only two days at home; but what a change there is in me. My brain is all confusion; and it might be a hundred years since I left school. This morning two strangers came to the house, demanding to see my father. They were rough hard men, whose voices sounded into my father's office, where he was busy writing, while I sat beside the fire, engaged in household sewing. I looked up at the loud noise of their voices, and saw him turn deadly pale, and bow his white-haired head upon his hands. But he went out in an instant, and returning with the strangers, bade me go to my sisters. I found Susannah in the parlour, looking scared and bewildered, and Priscilla in hysterics. After much ado they grew calmer, and when Priscilla was lying quiet on the sofa, and Susannah had sat down in mother's arm-chair to meditate, I crept back to my father's office, and rapping softly at the door, heard him say, "Come in." He was alone, and very sad.

"Father," I asked, "what is the matter?" and seeing his dear kind face, I flew to him.

"Eunice," he whispered very tenderly, "I will tell you all."

So then as I knelt at his knee, with my eyes fastened upon his, he told me a long history of troubles, every word of which removed my school-days farther and farther from me, and made them seem like the close of a finished life. The end of all was that these men were sent by his creditors to take possession of everything in our old home, where my mother had lived and died.

I caught my breath at first, as if I should go into hysterics like Priscilla, but I thought what good would that do for my father? So after a minute or two I was able to look up again bravely into his eyes. He then said he had his books to examine, so I kissed him, and came away.

In the parlour Priscilla was lying still, with her eyelids closed, and Susannah was quite lost in meditation. Neither of them noticed me entering or departing. I went into the kitchen to consult Jane about my father's dinner. She was rocking herself upon a chair, and rubbing her eyes red with her rough apron; and there in the elbow-chair which once belonged to my grandfather—all the Brethren knew George Fielding—sat one of the strangers, wearing a shaggy brown hat, from under which he was staring fixedly at a bag of dried herbs hanging to a hook in the ceiling. He did not bring his eyes down, even when I entered, and stood thunderstruck upon the door-sill; but he rounded up his large mouth, as if he were going to whistle.

"Good morning, sir," I said, as soon as I recovered myself; for my father had said we must regard these men only as the human instruments permitted to bring affliction to us; "will you please to tell me your name?"

The stranger fixed his eyes steadily upon me. After which he smiled a little to himself.

"John Robins is my name," he said, "and England is my nation, Woodbury is my dwelling-place, and Christ is my salvation."

He spake in a sing-song tone, and his eyes went up again to the bag of marjoram, twinkling as if with great satisfaction; and I pondered over his reply, until it became quite a comfort to me.

"I'm very glad to hear it," I said, at last, "because we are religious people, and I was afraid you might be different."

"Oh, I'll be no kind of nuisance, miss," he answered; "you make yourselves comfortable, and only bid Maria, here, to draw me my beer regular, and I'll not hurt your feelings."

"Thank you," I said. "Jane, you hear what Mr. Robins says. Bring some sheets down to air, and make up the bed in the Brothers' chamber. You'll find a bible and hymn-book on the table there, Mr. Robins." I was leaving the kitchen, when this singular man struck his clenched fist upon the dresser, with a noise which startled me greatly.

"Miss," he said, "don't you put yourself about; and if anybody else should ever put you out, about anything, remember John Robins of Woodbury. I'm your man for anything, whether in my line or out of my line; I am, by——"

He was about to add something more, but he paused suddenly, and his face grew a little more red, as he looked up again to the ceiling. So I left the kitchen.

I have since been helping my father with his books, being very thankful that I was always quick at sums.

P.S. I dreamed that the settlement was invaded by an army of men, led by John Robins, who insisted upon becoming our pastor.

November 10. I have been a journey of fifty miles, one half of it by stage-coach. I learned for the first time that my mother's brother, a worldly rich man, dwells fifteen miles beyond Woodbury. He does not belong to our people, and he was greatly displeased by my mother's marriage. It also appears that Susannah and Priscilla were not my mother's own daughters. My father had a little forlorn hope that our worldly kinsman might be inclined to help us in our great extremity; so I went forth with his blessings and prayers upon my errand. Brother More, who came over to see Priscilla yesterday,

met me at Woodbury Station, and saw me safely on the coach for my uncle's village. He is much older than I fancied; and his face is large, and coarse, and flabby-looking. I am surprised that Priscilla should betroth herself to him. However, he was very kind to me, and watched the coach out of the inn-yard; but almost before he was out of my sight, he was out of my mind, and I was considering what I should say to my uncle.

My uncle's house stands quite alone in the midst of meadows and groves of trees, all of which are leafless now, and waved to and fro in the damp and heavy air, like funeral plumes. I trembled greatly as I lifted the brass knocker, which had a grinning face upon it; and I let it fall with one loud single rap, which set all the dogs barking, and the rooks cawing in the tops of the trees. The servant conducted me across a low-roofed hall, to a parlour beyond: low-roofed also, but large and handsome, with a warm glow of crimson, which was pleasant to my eyes, after the grey gloom of the November day. It was already afternoon; and a tall fine-looking old man was lying comfortably upon a sofa fast asleep; while upon the other side of the hearth sat a dwarfed old lady, who lifted her fore-finger with a gesture of silence, and beckoned me to take a seat near the fire. I obeyed, and presently fell into a meditation.

At length a man's voice broke the silence, asking in a drowsy tone,

"What young lass is this?"

"I am Eunice Fielding," I replied, rising with reverence to the aged man, my uncle; and he gazed upon me with his keen grey eyes, until I was abashed, and a tear or two rolled down my cheeks in spite of myself, for my heart was very heavy.

"By Jove!" he exclaimed, "as like Sophy as two peas out of one pod!" and he laughed a short laugh, which, in my ears, lacked merriment. "Come here, Eunice," he added, "and kiss me."

Whereupon I walked gravely across the open space between us, and bent my face to his; but he would have me to sit upon his knee, and I, who had been at no time used to be fondled thus, even by my father, sat there uncomfortably.

"Well, my pretty one," said my uncle, "what is your errand and request to me? Upon my soul, I feel ready to promise thee anything."

As he spake, I bethought me of King Herod, and the sinful dancing-girl, and my heart sank within me; but at last I took courage, as did Esther the queen, and I made known my urgent business to him, telling him, even with tears, that my father was threatened with a prison, if he could find none to befriend him.

"Eunice," said my uncle, after a very long silence, "I will make a bargain with you and your father. He stole away my favourite sister from me, and I never saw her face again. I've no children, and I'm a rich man. If your father will give you up to me, keeping no claim upon you—even to never seeing your face again, if I so will it—then I will pay all his debts, and adopt you as my own daughter."

Before he could finish all these words, I sprang away from him, feeling more angered than I had ever done in my life.

"It could never be," I cried. "My father could never give me up, and I will never leave him."

"Be in no hurry to decide, Eunice," he said; "your father has two other daughters. I will give you an hour to reflect."

Upon that he and his wife left me alone in the pleasant room. My mind was firmly made up from the beginning. But as I sat before the glowing fire, it seemed as if all the bleak cold days of the coming winter trooped up and gathered round me, chilling the warm atmosphere of the room, and touching me with icy fingers, until I trembled like a coward. So I opened my little lot-book, which our pastor had given unto me, and I looked anxiously at the many slips of paper it contained. Many times I had drawn a lot from it, and found but vague counsel and comfort. But I now drew therefrom again, and the words upon the lot were, "Be of good courage!" Then I was greatly strengthened.

When the hour was ended, my uncle returned, and urged me with many worldly persuasions and allurements, mingled with threatenings, until at length I grew bold to answer him according to his snares.

"It is an evil thing," I said, "to tempt a child to forsake her father. Providence has put it into your power to lessen the sorrows of your fellow-creatures, but you seek to add to them. I would rather dwell with my father in a jail, than with you in a palace."

I turned and left him, finding my way out through the hall into the deepening twilight. It was more than a mile from the village through which the coach passed; and the hedge-banks rose high on each side of the deep lane. Though I walked very swiftly, the night came on before I had proceeded far from my uncle's house, with such thick gloom and fog that I could almost feel the darkness. "Be of good courage, Eunice!" said I; and to drive away the fears which lay in wait for me if I yielded but a little, I lifted up my voice, and began to sing our Evening Hymn.

Suddenly a voice a little way before me, took up the tune, in a clear deep rich tone, like that of the Brother who taught us music in the Settlement. As I stopped instantly, my heart leaping up with fear and a strange gladness, the voice before me ceased singing also.

"Good night," it said. There was such kindness and frankness and sweetness in the voice, that I trusted it at once.

"Wait for me," I said; "I am lost in the night, and I want to find my way to Longville."

"I am going there too," said the voice, to which I drew nearer each moment; and immediately I saw a tall dark figure in the mist beside me.

"Brother," I said, trembling a little, though wherefore I knew not. "are we far from Longville?"

"Only ten minutes' walk," he answered, in a blithe tone, which cheered me not a little. "Take my arm, and we shall soon be there."

As my hand rested on his arm lightly, I felt a sense of great support and protection. As we came near the lighted window of the village inn, we looked into one another's faces. His was pleasant and handsome, like some of the best pictures I have ever seen. I do not know why, but I thought of the Angel Gabriel.

"We are at Longville," he said; "tell me where I can take you to."

"Sir," I answered, for I could not say Brother to him in the light; "I wish first to get to Woodbury."

"To Woodbury," he repeated, "at this time of night, and alone! There is a return coach coming up in a few minutes, by which I travel to Woodbury. Will you accept of my escort there?"

"Sir, I thank you," I answered; and I stood silent beside him, until the coach lamps shone close upon us in the fog. The stranger opened the door, but I hung back with a foolish feeling of shame at my poverty, which it was needful to conquer.

"We are poor people," I stammered. "I must travel outside."

"Not such a winter's night as this," he said. "Jump in."

"No, no," I replied, recovering my senses, "I shall go outside." A decent country woman, with a child, were already seated on the top of the coach, and I quickly followed them. My seat was the outer one, and hung over the wheels. The darkness was so dense that the fitful glimmer of the coach-lamps upon the leafless hedge-rows was the only light to be seen. All else was black, pitchy night. I could think of nothing but my father, and the jail opening to imprison him. Presently I felt a hand laid firmly on my arm, and Gabriel's voice spake to me:

"Your seat is a dangerous one," he said. "A sudden jerk might throw you off."

"I am so miserable," I sobbed, all my courage breaking down; and in the darkness I buried my face in my hands, and wept silently; and even as I wept, the bitterness of my sorrow was assuaged.

"Brother," I said—for in the darkness I could call him so again. "I am only just come home from school, and I have not learned the ways and troubles of the world yet."

"My child," he answered, in a low tone, "I saw you lean your head upon your hands and weep. Can I be of any help to you?"

"No," I replied; "the sorrow belongs to me only, and to my house."

He said no more, but I felt his arm stretched out to form a barrier across the space where I might have fallen; and so through the black night we rode on to Woodbury.

Brother More was awaiting me at the coach-office. He hurried me away, scarcely giving me time to glance at Gabriel, who stood looking after me. He was eager to hear of my interview with my uncle; when I told him of my failure, he grew thoughtful, saying little until I was in the railway carriage, when he leaned forward and whispered, "Tell Priscilla I will come over in the morning."

Brother More is a rich man; perhaps, for Priscilla's sake, he will free my father.

Nov. 11. I dreamed last night that Gabriel stood beside me, saying, "I come to bring thee glad tidings." But as I listened eagerly, he sighed, and vanished away.

Nov. 15. Brother More is here every day, but he says nothing about helping my father. If help does not come soon, he will be cast into prison. Peradventure, my uncle will relent, and offer us some easier terms. If it were only to live half my time with him, I would consent to dwell in his house, even as Daniel and the three children dwelt unharmed in the court of Babylon. I will write to him to that effect.

Nov. 19. No answer from my uncle. To-day, going to Woodbury with Priscilla, who wished to converse with the pastor of the church there, I spent the hour she was engaged with him in finding my way to the jail, and walking round the outside of its gloomy and massive walls. I felt very mournful and faint-hearted, thinking of my poor father. At last, being very weary, I sat down on the step at the gateway, and looked into my little lot-book again. Once more I drew the verse, "Be of good courage." Just then, Brother More and Priscilla appeared. There was a look upon his face which I disliked, but I remembered that he was to be my sister's husband, and I rose and offered him my hand, which he tucked up under his arm, his fat hand resting upon it. So we three walked to and fro under the prison walls. Suddenly, in a garden sloping away beneath us, I perceived him whom I call Gabriel (not knowing any other name), with a fair sweet-looking young woman at his side. I could not refrain from weeping, for what reason I cannot tell, unless it be my father's affairs. Brother More returned home with us, and sent John Robins away. John Robins desired me to remember him, which I will as long as I live.

Nov. 20. Most miserable day. My poor father is in jail. At dinner-time to-day two most evil-looking men arrested him. God forgive me for wishing they were dead! Yet my father spake very patiently and gently.

"Send for Brother More," he said, after a pause, "and act according to his counsel."

So after a little while they carried him away. What am I to do?

Nov. 30. Late last night we were still discoursing as to our future plans. Priscilla thinks Brother More will hasten their marriage, and Susannah has an inward assurance that the lot will fall to her to be Brother Schmidt's wife.

She spake wisely of the duties of a missionary's life, and of the grace needed to fulfil them. But I could think of nothing but my father trying to sleep within the walls of the jail.

Brother More says he thinks he can see a way to release my father, only we are all to pray that we may have grace to conquer our self-will. I am sure I am willing to do anything, even to selling myself into slavery, as some of our first missionaries did in the slave-times in the West Indies. But in England one cannot sell one's self, though I would be a very faithful servant. I want to get at once a sum large enough to pay our debts. Brother More bids me not spoil my eyes with crying.

Dec. 1. The day on which my father was arrested, I made a last appeal to my uncle. This morning I had a brief note from him, saying he had commissioned his lawyer to visit me, and state the terms on which he was willing to aid me. Even as I read it, his lawyer desired to see me alone. I went to the parlour, trembling with anxiety. It was no other than Gabriel who stood before me, and I took heart, remembering my dream that he appeared to me, saying, "I come to bring thee glad tidings."

"Miss Eunice Fielding," he said, in his pleasant voice, and looking down upon me with a smile which seemed to shed sunshine upon my sad and drooping spirit.

"Yes," I answered, my eyes falling foolishly before his; and I beckoned to him to resume his seat, while I stood leaning against my mother's great arm-chair.

"I have a hard message for you," said Gabriel; "your uncle has dictated this paper, which must be signed by you and your father. He will release Mr. Fielding, and settle one hundred pounds a year upon him, on condition that he will retire to some German Moravian settlement, and that you will accept the former terms."

"I cannot," I cried bitterly. "Oh! sir, ought I to leave my father?"

"I am afraid not," he answered, in a low voice.

"Sir," I said, "you must please say 'no' to my uncle."

"I will," he replied, "and make it sound as gently as I can. You have a friend in me, Miss Eunice."

His voice lingered upon Eunice, as if it were no common name to him, but something rare and pleasing. I never heard it spoken so pleasantly before. After a little while he rose to take his leave.

"Brother," I said, giving him my hand, "farewell."

"I shall see you again, Miss Eunice," he answered.

He saw me again sooner than he expected, for I travelled by the next train to Woodbury, and, as I left the dark carriage in which I journeyed, I saw him alight from another part of the train, and at the same instant his eyes fell upon me.

" Where are you going to now, Eunice ?" he demanded.

It seemed a pleasanter greeting than if he had called me Miss. I told him I knew my way to the jail, for that I had been not long ago to look at the outside of it. I saw the tears stand in his eyes, but, without speaking, he drew my hand through his arm, and I silently, but with a very lightened heart, walked beside him to the great portal of my father's prison.

We entered a square court, with nothing to be seen save the grey winter sky lying, as it were flat, overhead ; and there was my father, pacing to and fro, with his arms crossed upon his breast and his head bowed down, as if it would never be raised again. I cried aloud, and ran and fell on his neck, and knew nothing more until I opened my eyes in a small bare room, and felt my father holding me in his arms, and Gabriel kneeling before me, chafing my hands, and pressing his lips upon them.

Afterwards Gabriel and my father conferred together ; but before long Brother More arrived, whereupon Gabriel departed. Brother More said, solemnly :

" That man is a wolf in sheep's clothing, and our Eunice is a tender lamb."

I cannot believe that Gabriel is a wolf.

Dec. 2. I have taken a room in a cottage near the jail, the abode of John Robins and his wife, a decent tidy woman. So I can spend every day with my father.

Dec. 13. My father has been in prison a whole fortnight. Brother More went over to see Priscilla last night, and this morning he is to lay before us his plan for my father's release. I am going to meet him at the jail.

When I entered the room, my father and Brother More looked greatly perturbed, and my poor father leaned back in his chair, as if exhausted after a long conflict.

" Speak to her, brother," he said.

Then Brother More told us of a heavenly vision which had appeared to him, directing him to break off his betrothal to Priscilla, and to take me— me !—for his wife. After which he awoke, and these words abode in his mind, " The dream is certain, and the interpretation thereof sure."

" Therefore, Eunice," he said, in an awful voice, " do you and Priscilla see to it, lest you should be found fighting against the Lord."

I was struck dumb as with a great shock, but I heard him add these words :

" I was also instructed in the vision, to set your father free, upon the day that you become my wife."

" But," I said at last, my whole heart recoiling from him, " this would be a shameful wrong to Priscilla. It cannot be a vision from Heaven, but a delusion and snare. Marry Priscilla, and set my father free ? Surely, surely, it was a lying vision."

" No," he said, fastening his gaze upon me ; " I chose Priscilla rashly of my own judgment. Therein I erred ; but I have promised her half her dowry as a compensation for my error."

" Father," I cried, " surely I ought to have some direction also, as well as he. Why should only he have a vision ?" Then I added that I would go home and see Priscilla, and seek a sign for my own guidance.

December 14. Priscilla was ill in bed when I reached home, and refused to see me. I arose at five o'clock this morning, and stole down into the parlour. As I lighted the lamp, the parlour looked forlorn and deserted, and yet there lingered about it a ghostly feeling, as if perhaps my mother, and the dead children whom I never saw, had been sitting on the hearth in the night, as we sat in the daytime. Maybe she knew of my distress, and had left some tokens for my comfort and counsel. My Bible lay upon the table, but it was closed ; her angel fingers had not opened it upon any verse that might have guided me. There was no mode of seeking direction, save by casting of lots.

I cut three little slips of paper of one length, and exactly similar—three, though surely I only needed two. Upon the first I wrote, " To be Brother More's wife," and upon the second, " To be a Single Sister." The third lay upon the desk, blank and white, as if waiting for some name to be written upon it, and suddenly all the chilly cold of the winter morning passed into a sultry heat, until I threw open the casement, and let the frosty air breathe upon my face. I said in my own heart I would leave myself a chance, though my conscience smote me for that word " chance." So I laid the three slips of paper between the leaves of my Bible, and sat down opposite to them, afraid of drawing the lot which held the secret of my future life.

There was no mark to guide me in the choice of one slip of paper from another ; and I dared not stretch out my hand to draw one of them. For I was bound to abide by the solemn decision. It seemed too horrible to become Brother More's wife ; and to me the Sisters' Home, where the Single Sisters dwell, having all things in common, seems dreary and monotonous and somewhat desolate. But if I should draw the blank paper ! My heart fluttered ; again and again I stretched out my hand, and withdrew it ; until at last the oil in the lamp being spent, its light grew dimmer and dimmer, and, fearful of being still longer without guidance, I snatched the middle lot from between the leaves of my Bible. There was only a glimmer of dying light, by which I read the words, " To be Brother More's wife."

That is the last entry in my journal, written three years ago.

When Susannah came down stairs and entered the parlour, she found me sitting before my desk, almost in an idiotic state, with that miserable lot in my hand. There was no need to explain it to her ; she looked at the other slip of paper, one blank, and the other inscribed, " To be a Single Sister," and she knew I had been casting lots. I remember her crying over me a little, and kissing me with unaccustomed tenderness ; and then she returned to her chamber, and I heard her speaking to Priscilla in grave and sad tones. After that, we were all passive; even Priscilla was stolidly resigned. Brother More came over, and Susannah informed him of the irrevocable lot which I had drawn; but besought him to refrain from seeing me that day; and he left me alone to grow somewhat used to the sense of my wretchedness.

Early the next morning I returned to Woodbury; my only consolation being the thought that my dear father would be set free, and might live with me in wealth and comfort all the rest of his life. During the succeeding days I scarcely left his side, never suffering Brother More to be alone with me; and morning and night John Robins or his wife accompanied me to the gate of the jail, and waited for me to return with them to their cottage.

My father was to be set free, only on my wedding-day, and the marriage was hurried on. Many of Priscilla's store of wedding garments were suitable for me. Every hour brought my doom nearer.

One morning, in the gloom and twilight of a December dawn, I suddenly met Gabriel in my path. He spake rapidly and earnestly, but I scarcely knew what he said, and I answered, falteringly:.

"I am going to be married to Brother Joshua More on New Year's-day, and he will then release my father."

"Eunice," he cried, standing before me in the narrow path, "you can never marry him. I know the fat hypocrite. Good Heaven! I love you a hundred times better than he does. Love! The rascal does not know what it means."

I answered not a word, for I felt afraid both of myself and him, though I did not believe Gabriel to be a wolf in sheep's clothing.

"Do you know who I am?" he asked.

"No," I whispered.

"I am your uncle's nephew by marriage," he said, "and I have been brought up in his house. Break off this wicked marriage with the fellow More, and I will engage to release your father. I am young, and can work. I will pay your father's debts."

"It is impossible," I replied. "Brother More has had a heavenly vision, and I have drawn the lot. There is no hope. I must marry him upon New Year's-day."

Then Gabriel persuaded me to tell him the whole story of my trouble. He laughed a little, and bade me be of good comfort; and I could not make him understand how impossible it was that I should contend against the dispensation of the lot.

Always when I was with my father I strove to conceal my misery, talking to him of the happy days we should spend together some time. Likewise I sang within the walls of the prison, the simple hymns which we had been wont to sing in the peaceful church at school amid a congregation of serene hearts, and I strengthened

my own heart and my father's by the recollected counsels of my dear lost pastor. Thus my father guessed little of my hidden suffering, and looked forward with hope to the day that would throw open his prison doors.

Once I went to the pastor, dwelling in Woodbury, and poured out my heart to him—save that I made no mention of Gabriel—and he told me it was often thus with young girls before their marriage, but that I had a clear leading; he also told me that Brother More was a devout man, and I should soon love and reverence him as my husband.

At length the last day of the year came; a great day among our people, when we drew our lot for the following year. Everything seemed at an end. All hope fled from me, if there ever had been any hope in my heart. I left my father early in the evening, for I could no longer conceal my wretchedness; yet when I was outside the prison walls I wandered to and fro, hovering about it, as if these days, miserable as they had been, were happy to those which were drawing near. Brother More had not been near us all day, but doubtless he was busy in his arrangements to release my father. I was still lingering under the great walls, when a carriage drove up noiselessly—for the ground was sprinkled with soft snow—and Gabriel sprang out, and almost clasped me in his arms.

"My dear Eunice," he said, "you must come with me at once. Our uncle will save you from this hateful marriage."

I do not know what I should have done had not John Robins called out from the driver's seat, "All right, Miss Eunice; remember John Robins."

Upon that I left myself in Gabriel's hands, and he lifted me into the carriage, wrapping warm coverings about me. It seemed to me no other than a happy dream, as we drove noiselessly along snowy roads, with the pale wan light of the young moon falling upon the white country, and now and then shining upon the face of Gabriel, as he leaned forward from time to time to draw the wrappers closer round me.

We might have been three hours on the way, when we turned into a by-road, which presently I recognised as the deep lane wherein I had first met Gabriel. We were going then to my uncle's house. So with a lightened heart I stepped out of the carriage, and entered his doors for the second time.

Gabriel conducted me into the parlour which I had seen before, and placed me in a chair upon the hearth, removing my shawl and bonnet with a pleasant and courteous care; and he was standing opposite to me, regarding me with a smile upon his handsome face, when the door opened and my uncle entered.

"Come and kiss me, Eunice," he said; and I obeyed him wonderingly.

"Child," he continued, stroking my hair back from my face, "you would not come to me of your own will, so I commissioned this young fellow to kidnap you. We are not going to have you marry Joshua More. I cannot do with him as my nephew. Let him marry Priscilla."

There was such a hearty tone in my uncle's voice, that for a moment I felt comforted, though I knew that he could not set aside my lot. So he seated me beside him, while I still looked with wonderment into his face.

"I am going to draw a lot for you," he said, with an air of merriment; "what would my little rosebud say to her fat suitor, if she knew that her father was a freed man at this moment?"

◦ I dared not look into his face or into Gabriel's. For I remembered that I myself had sought for a token; and that no earthly power could set aside that, or the heavenly vision also, which Brother More had seen.

"Uncle," I said, shuddering, "I have no voice in this matter. I drew the lot fairly, and I must abide by it. You cannot help me."

"We will see," he answered; "it is New Year's-eve, you know, and time to draw again. The lot will neither be to become Brother More's wife, nor a Single Sister, I promise you. We shall draw the blank this time!"

While I yet wondered at these words, I heard a sound of footsteps in the hall, and the door opened, and my beloved father stood upon the threshold, stretching out his arms to me. How he came there I knew not; but I flew to him with a glad cry, and hid my face upon his breast.

"You are welcome, Mr. Fielding," said my uncle; "Phil!"—it did now appear that Gabriel's name was Philip—"bring Mr. More this way."

I started with fright and wonder, and my father also looked troubled, and drew me nearer to his side. Brother More entered with a cowardly and downcast mien, which made him appear a hundred-fold more repulsive in my eyes, as he stood near the door, with his craven face turned towards us.

"Mr. More," said my uncle, "I believe you are to marry my niece, Eunice Fielding, to-morrow?"

"I did not know she was your niece," he answered, in an abject tone. "I would not have presumed——"

"But the heavenly vision, Mr. More?" interrupted my uncle.

He looked round for a moment, with a spiritless glance, and his eyes sank.

"It was a delusion," he muttered.

"It was a lie!" said Gabriel.

"Mr. More," continued my uncle, "if the heavenly vision be true, it will cost you the sum of five thousand five hundred pounds, the amount in which you are indebted to me, with sundry sums due to my nephew here. Yet if it be true, you must abide by it, of course."

"It was not true," he answered; "the vision was concerning Priscilla, to whom I was betrothed. I was ensnared to change the name to that of Eunice."

"Then go and marry Priscilla," said my uncle, good humouredly. "Philip, take him away."

But Priscilla would have no more to do with Brother More, and shortly afterwards she settled among the Single Sisters in the same settlement where I had lived my quiet and peaceful youth. Her store of wedding garments, which had been altered to fit me, came in at last for Susannah, who was chosen to be the wife of Brother Schmidt, according to her inward assurance; and she went out to join him in the West Indies, from whence she writes many happy letters. I was troubled for a time about my lot, but certainly if Brother More's vision was concerning Priscilla, I could not be required to abide by it. Moreover, I never saw him again. My uncle and father, who had never met before, formed a close friendship, and my uncle would hear of nothing but that we should dwell together in his large mansion, where I might be as a daughter unto both of them. People say we have left the Church of the United Brethren; but it is not so. Only, as I had found one evil man within it, so also I have found some good men without it.

Gabriel is not one of the Brethren.

V.

TO BE TAKEN IN WATER.

Minnie, my blessed little wife, and I, had been just one month married. We had returned only two days from our honeymoon tour at Killarney. I was a junior partner in the firm of Schwarzmoor and Laddock, bankers, Lombard-street (I must conceal real names), and I had four days more of my leave of absence still to enjoy. I was supremely happy in my bright new cottage south-west of London, and was revelling in delicious idleness on that bright October morning, watching the great yellow leaves fall in the sunshine. Minnie sat by me under the hawthorn-tree; otherwise, I should not have been supremely happy.

Little Betsy, Minnie's maid, came fluttering down the garden with an ominous-looking letter in her hand.

It was a telegram from Mr. Schwarzmoor. It contained only these words:

"We want you to start to the Continent directly with specie. Neapolitan loan. No delay. Transactions of great importance since you left. Sorry to break up holiday. Be at office by 6.30. Start from London Bridge by 9.15, and catch Dover night boat."

"Is the boy gone?"

"Boy did not leave it, sir. Elderly gentleman, going to Dawson's, brought it. The office boy was out, and the gentleman happened to be coming past our house."

"Herbert dear, you won't go, you mustn't go," said Minnie, leaning on my shoulder, and bending down her face. "Don't go."

"I must, my dearest. The firm has no one to

trust to, but me, in such a case. It is but a week's absence. I must start in ten minutes, and catch the 4.20 on its way up."

"That was a very important telegram," I said sharply to the station-master, "and you ought not to have sent it by any unknown and unauthorised person. Who *was* this old gentleman, pray ?"

"Who was it, Harvey ?" said the station-master, rather sulkily, to the porter.

"Old gent, sir, very respectable, as comes to the Dawsons', the training-stables. Has horses there."

"Do not let that sort of thing occur again, Mr. Jennings," I said, "or I shall be obliged to report it. I wouldn't have had that telegram mislaid, for a hundred pounds."

Mr. Jennings, the station-master, grumbled something, and then boxed the telegraph boy's ears. Which seemed to do him (Mr. Jennings) good.

"We were getting very anxious," said Mr. Schwarzmoor, as I entered the bank parlour, only three minutes late. "Very anxious, weren't we, Goldrick ?"

"Very anxious," said the little neat head clerk. "Very anxious."

Mr. Schwarzmoor was a full faced man of about sixty, with thick white eyebrows and a red face —a combination which gave him an expression of choleric old age. He was a shrewd severe man of business : a little impetuous and fond of rule, but polite, kind, and considerate.

"I hope your charming wife is quite well. Sorry, indeed, to break up your holiday ; but no help for it, my dear fellow. There is the specie in those two iron boxes, enclosed in leather to look like samples. They are fastened with letter-locks, and contain a quarter of a million in gold. The Neapolitan king apprehends a rebellion." (It was three years before Garibaldi's victories.) "You will take the money to Messrs. Pagliavicini and Rossi, No. 172 Toledo, Naples. The names that open the locks are, on the one with the white star on the cover, Masinisa ; on the one with the black star, Cotopaxo. Of course you will not forget the talismanic words. Open the boxes at Lyons, to make sure that all is safe. Talk to no one. Make no friends on the road. Your commission is of vast importance."

"I shall pass," said I, "for a commercial traveller."

"Pardon me for my repeated cautions, Blamyre, but I am an older man than you, and know the danger of travelling with specie. If your purpose was known to-night in Paris, your road to Marseilles would be as dangerous as if all the galley-slaves at Toulon had been let loose in special chase of you. I do not doubt your discretion : I only warn you to be careful. Of course, you go armed ?"

I opened my coat, and showed a belt under my waistcoat, with a revolver in it. At which war-like spectacle the old clerk drew back in alarm.

"Good !" said Mr. Schwarzmoor. "But one grain of prudence is worth five times the five

bullets in those five barrels. You will stop in Paris to-morrow to transact business with Lefebre and Desjeans, and you will go on by the 12.15 (night) to Marseilles, catching the boat on Friday. We will telegraph to you at Marseilles. Are the letters for Paris ready, Mr. Hargrave ?"

"Yes, sir, nearly ready. Mr. Wilkins is hard at them."

I reached Dover by midnight, and instantly engaged four porters to carry my specie chests down the stone steps leading from the pier to the Calais boat. The first was taken on board quite safely ; but while the second was being carried down, one of the men slipped, and would certainly have fallen into the water, had he not been caught in the arms of a burly old Indian officer, who, laden with various traps, and urging forward his good-natured but rather vulgar wife, was preceding me.

"Steady there, my lad," he said. "Why, what have you got there ? Hardware ?"

"Don't know, sir ; I only know it's heavy enough to break any man's back," was the rough answer, as the man thanked his questioner in his blunt way.

"These steps, sir, are very troublesome for bringing down heavy goods," said an obliging voice behind me. "I presume, sir, from your luggage, that we are of the same profession ?"

I looked round as we just then stepped on board. The person who addressed me was a tall thin man, with a long and rather Jewish nose, and a narrow elongated face. He wore a great-coat too short for him, a flowered waistcoat, tight trousers, a high shirt collar, and a light sprigged stiff neckcloth.

I replied that I *had* the honour to be a commercial traveller, and that I thought we were going to have a rough night of it.

"Decidedly dirty night," he replied ; "and I advise you, sir, to secure a berth at once. The boat, I see, is very crowded."

I went straight to my berth, and lay down for an hour ; at the end of that time I got up and looked around me. At one of the small tables sat half a dozen of the passengers, including the old Indian and my old-fashioned interrogator. They were drinking bottled porter, and appeared very sociable. I rose and joined them, and we exchanged some remarks not complimentary to night travelling.

"By Jove, sir, it is simply unbearable !" said the jovial Major Baxter (for he soon told us his name) ; "it is as stifling as Peshawah when the hot Tinsang wind is blowing ; suppose we three go on deck and take a little air ? My wife suffers in these crossings ; she's invisible, I know, till the boat stops. Steward, bring up some more bottled porter."

When we got on deck, I saw, to my extreme surprise, made conspicuous by their black and white stars, four other cases exactly similar to mine, except that they had no painted brand upon them. I could hardly believe my eyes ; but there they were ; leather covers, letter-locks, and all.

"Those cases are mine, sir," remarked Mr. Levison (I knew my fellow-commercial's name from the captain's having addressed him by it). "I am travelling for the house of Mackintosh. Those cases contain waterproof paletots, the best made. Our house has used such cases for forty years. It is sometimes inconvenient, this accidental resemblance of luggage—leads to mistakes. Your goods are much heavier than my goods, as I judge? Gas improvements, railway chairs, cutlery, or something else in iron?"

I was silent, or I made some vague reply.

"Sir," said Levison, "I augur well of your future; trade secrets should be kept inviolate. Don't you think so, sir?"

The major thus appealed to, replied, "Sir, by Jove, you're right! One cannot be too careful in these days. Egad, sir, the world is a mass of deceit."

"There's Calais light!" cried some one at that moment; and there it was, straight ahead, casting sparkles of comfort over the dark water.

I thought no more of my travelling companions. We parted at Paris: I went my way and they went their way. The major was going to pay a visit at Dromont, near Lyons; thence he would go to Marseilles en route for Alexandria. Mr. Levison was bound for Marseilles, like myself and the major—but not by my train—at least he feared not—as he had much to do in Paris.

I had transacted my business in the French capital, and was on my way to the Palais Royal, with M. Lefebre fils, a great friend of mine. It was about six o'clock, and we were crossing the Rue St. Honoré, when there passed us a tall Jewish-looking person, in a huge white mackintosh, whom I recognised as Mr. Levison. He was in a hired open carriage, and his four boxes were by his side. I bowed to him, but he did not seem to notice me.

"Eh bien! That drôle, who is that?" said my friend, with true Parisian superciliousness.

I replied that it was only a fellow-passenger, who had crossed with me the night before.

In the very same street I ran up against the major and his wife, on their way to the railway station.

"Infernal city, this," said the major; "smells so of onion. I should like, if it was mine, to wash it out, house by house; 'tain't wholesome, 'pon my soul 'tain't wholesome. Julia, my dear, this is my pleasant travelling companion of last night. By-the-by, just saw that commercial traveller! Sharp business man that: no sight-seeing about him. Bourse and bank all day,—senior partner some day."

"And how many more?" said my friend Lefebre, when we shook hands and parted with the jolly major. "That is a good boy—he superabounds—he overflows—but he is one of your epicurean lazy officers, I am sure. Your army, it must be reformed, or India will slip from you like a handful of sand—vous verrez, mon cher."

Midnight came, and I was standing at the ter-

minus, watching the transport of my luggage, when a cab drove up, and an Englishman leaping out asked the driver in excellent French for change for a five-franc piece. It was Levison; but I saw no more of him, for the crowd just then pushed me forward

I took my seat with only two other persons in the carriage—two masses of travelling cloak and capote—two bears, for all I could see to the contrary.

Once away from the lights of Paris, and in the pitch dark country, I fell asleep and dreamed of my dear little wife, and our dear little home. Then a feeling of anxiety ran across my mind. I dreamed that I had forgotten the words with which to open the letter-locks. I ransacked mythology, history, science, in vain. Then I was in the banking parlour at No. 172 Toledo, Naples, threatened with instant death by a file of soldiers, if I did not reveal the words, or explain where the boxes had been hid; for I had hidden them for some inscrutable no reason. At that moment an earthquake shook the city, a flood of fire rolled past beneath the window, Vesuvius had broken loose and was upon us. I cried in my agony—"Gracious Heaven, reveal to me those words!" when I awoke.

"Dromont! Dromont! Dix minutes d'arrête, messieurs."

Half blinded with the sudden light, I stumbled to the buffet, and asked for a cup of coffee, when three or four noisy young English tourists came hurrying in, surrounding a quiet imperturbable elderly commercial traveller. It was actually Levison again! They led him along in triumph, and called for champagne.

"Yes! yes!" the leader said. "You must have some, old fellow. We have won three games, you know, and you held such cards, too. Come along, look alive, you fellow with the nightcap, —Cliquot—gilt top, you duffer. You shall have your revenge before we get to Lyons, old chap."

Levison chattered good humouredly about the last game, and took the wine. In a few minutes the young men had drunk their champagne, and had gone out to smoke. In another moment Levison caught my eye.

"Why, good gracious," he said, "who'd have thought of this! Well, I am glad to see you. Now, my dear sir, you must have some champagne with me. Here, another bottle, monsieur, if you please. I hope, long before we get to Lyons, to join you, my dear sir. I am tired of the noise of those youngsters. Besides, I object to high stakes, on principle."

The moment the waiter brought the champagne, Levison took the bottle.

"No," he said; "I never allow any one to open wine for me." He turned his back from me to remove the wire; removed it; and was filling my glass; when up dashed a burly hearty man to shake hands with me—so awkward in his heartiness that he broke the champagne bottle. Not a drop of the wine was saved. It was the major—hot as usual, and in a tremendous bustle.

"By Jove, sir; dooced sorry. Let me order

another bottle. How are you, gentlemen? Lucky, indeed, to meet you both again. Julia's with the luggage. We can be very cozy together. More champagne here. What's bottle in French? Most shameful thing! Those French friends of Julia's were gone off to Biarritz, pretending to have forgotten that we were coming—after six weeks with us in London, too! Precious shabby, not to put too fine a point upon it. By Jove, sir, there's the bell. We'll all go in the same carriage: They will not bring that champagne."

Levison looked rather annoyed. "I shall not see you," he said, "for a station or two. I must join those boys, and let them give me my revenge. Cleared me out of twenty guineas! I have not been so imprudent since I was first on the road. Good-bye, Major Baxter—goodbye, Mr. Blamyre!"

I wondered how this respectable old fellow, who so keenly relished his game at whist, had got hold of my name; but I remembered in a moment that he must have seen the direction on my luggage.

Flashes of crimson and green lights, a shout from some pointsman, a glimpse of rows of poplars, and lines of suburban houses, and we once more plunged into the yielding darkness.

I found the major very droll and pleasant, but evidently ruled by his fussy, good-natured, managing, masculine wife. He was full of stories of bungalows, compounds, and the hills; in all of which narrations he was perpetually interrupted by Mrs. Baxter.

"By Jove, sir!" he said, "I wish I could sell out, and go into your line of business. I am almost sick of India—it deranges one's liver so infernally."

"Now, John, how can you go on so! You know you never had a day's illness in all your life, except that week when you smoked out a whole box of Captain Mason's cheroots."

"Well, I pulled through it, Julia," said the major, striking himself a tremendous blow on the chest; "but I've been an unlucky devil as to promotion—always bad luck in everything. If I bought a horse, it made a point of going lame next day; never went in a train but it broke down."

"Now don't, John; pray don't go on so," said Mrs. Baxter, "or I shall really be very angry. Such nonsense! You'll get your step in time. Be patient, like me, major; take things more quietly. I hope you put a direction on that hat-box of yours? Where is the sword-case? If it wasn't for me, major, you'd get to Suez with nothing but the coat on your back."

Just then, the train stopped at Charmont, and in tripped Levison, with his white mackintosh over his arm, and his bundle of umbrellas and sticks.

"No more sovereign points for me!" he said, producing a pack of cards. "But if you and the major and Mrs. Baxter would like a rubber—shilling points—I'm for you. Cut for partners."

We assented with pleasure. We cut for partners. I and Mrs. Baxter against the major

and Levison. We won nearly every game. Levison played too cautiously, and the major laughed, talked, and always forgot what cards were out.

Still it killed the time; the red and black turned up, changed, and ran into remarkable sequences; and the major's flukes and extraordinary luck in holding (not in playing) cards amused us, we laughed at Levison's punctilious care, and at Mrs. Baxter's avarice for tricks, and were as pleasant a party as the dim lamp of a night-train ever shone on. I could think of little, nevertheless, but my precious boxes.

There we were rushing through France, seeing nothing, heeding nothing, and having as little to do with our means of transit as if we had been four Arabian princes, seated on a flying enchanted carpet.

The game gradually grew more intermittent, the conversation more incessant. Levison, stiff of neckcloth as ever, and imperturbable and punctilious as ever, became chatty. He grew communicative about his business.

"I have at last," he said, in his precise and measured voice, "after years of attention to the subject, discovered the great secret which the waterproofers have so long coveted; how to let out the heated air of the body, and yet at the same time to exclude the rain. On my return to London, I offer this secret to the Mackintosh firm for ten thousand pounds; if they refuse the offer, I at once open a shop in Paris, call the new fabric Magentosh, in honour of the emperor's great Italian victory, and sit down and quietly realise a cool million—that's my way!"

"That's the real business tone," said the major, admiringly.

"Ah, major," cried his wife, ever ready to improve a subject, "if you had only had a little of Mr. Levison's prudence and energy, then, indeed, you'd have been colonel of your regiment before this."

Mr. Levison then turned the conversation to the subject of locks.

"I always use the letter-lock myself," he said. "My two talismanic words are TURLURETTE and PAPAGAYO—two names I once heard in an old French farce—who could guess them? It would take the adroitest thief seven hours to decipher even one. You find letter-locks safe, sir?" (He turned to me.)

I replied dryly that I did, and asked what time our train was due at Lyons.

"We are due at Lyons at 4.30," said the major; "it is now five to four. I don't know how it is, but I have a sort of presentiment tonight of some break-down. I am always in for it. When I went tiger-hunting, it was always my elephant that the beast pinned. If some of us were ordered up to an unhealthy out-of-the-way fort, it was always my company. It may be superstitious, I own, but I feel we shall have a break-down before we get to Marseilles. How fast we're going! Only see how the carriage rocks!"

I unconsciously grew nervous, but I concealed it. Could the major be a rogue, planning some scheme against me? But no: his red bluff face, and his clear good-natured guileless eyes, refuted the suspicion.

"Nonseuse, be quiet, major; that's the way you always make a journey disagreeable," said his wife, arranging herself for sleep. Then Levison began talking about his early life, and how, in George the Fourth's time, he was travelling for a cravat house in Bond-street. He grew eloquent in favour of the old costume.

"Low Radical fellows," he said, "run down the first gentleman in Europe, as he was justly called. I respect his memory. He was a wit, and the friend of wits; he was lavishly generous, and disdained poor pitiful economy. He dressed well, sir; he looked well, sir; he was a gentleman of perfect manners. Sir, this is a slovenly and shabby age. When I was young, no gentleman ever travelled without at least two dozen cravats, four whalebone stiffeners, and an iron to smooth the tie, and produce a thin equal edge to the muslin. There were no less, sir, than eighteen modes of putting on the cravat; there was the cravate à la Diane, the cravate à l'Anglaise, the cravate au nœud Gordien, the cravate——"

The train jolted, moved on, slackened, stopped.

The major thrust his head out of window, and shouted to a passing guard:

"Where are we?"

"Twenty miles from Lyons—Fort Rouge, monsieur."

"What is the matter? Anything the matter?"

An English voice answered from the next window:

"A wheel broken, they tell us. We shall have to wait two hours, and transfer the luggage."

"Good Heaven!" I could not help exclaiming.

Levison put his head out of window. "It is but too true," he said, drawing it in again; "two hours' delay at least, the man says. Tiresome, very—but such things will happen on the road; take it coolly. We'll have some coffee and another rubber. We must each look to our own luggage; or, if Mr. Blamyre goes in and orders supper, I'll see to it all. But, good gracious, what is that shining out there by the station lamps? Hei, monsieur!" (to a passing gendarme whom the major had hailed), "what is going on at the station?"

"Monsieur," said the gendarme, saluting, "those are soldiers of the First Chasseurs; they happened to be at the station on their way to Châlons; the station-master has sent them to surround the luggage-van, and see to the transfer of the baggage. No passenger is to go near it, as there are government stores of value in the train."

Levison spat on the ground and muttered excrations to himself:—I supposed at French railways.

"By Jove, sir, did you ever see such clumsy carts?" said Major Baxter, pointing to two country carts, each with four strong horses, that were drawn up under a hedge close to the station; for we had struggled on as far as the first turn-table, some hundred yards from the first houses of the village of Fort Rouge.

Levison and I tried very hard to get near our luggage, but the soldiers sternly refused our approach. It gave me some comfort, however, to see my chests transferred carefully, with many curses on their weight. I saw no sign of government stores, and I told the major so.

"Oh, they're sharp," he replied, "dooced sharp. Maybe the empress's jewels—one little package only, perhaps; but still not difficult to steal in a night confusion."

Just then there was a shrill piercing whistle, as if a signal. The horses in the two carts tore into a gallop, and flew out of sight.

"Savages, sir; mere barbarians still," exclaimed the major; "unable to use railways even now we've given them to them."

"Major!" said his wife, in a voice of awful reproof, "spare the feelings of these foreigners, and remember your position as an officer and a gentleman."

The major rubbed his hands, and laughed uproariously.

"A pack of infernal idiots," cried Levison; "they can do nothing without soldiers; soldiers here, soldiers there, soldiers everywhere."

"Well, these precautions are sometimes useful, sir," said Mrs. B.; "France is a place full of queer characters. The gentleman next you any day at a table d'hôte may be a returned convict. Major, you remember that case at Cairo three years ago?"

"Cairo, Julia my dear, is not in France."

"I know that, major, I hope. But the house was a French hotel, and that's the same thing." Mrs. B. spoke sharply.

"I shall have a nap, gentlemen. For my part, I'm tired," said the major, as we took our places in the Marseilles train, after three hours' tedious delay. "The next thing will be the boat breaking down, I suppose."

"Major, you wicked man, don't fly out against Providence," said his wife.

Levison grew eloquent again about the Prince Regent, his diamond epaulettes, and his inimitable cravats; but Levison's words seemed to lengthen, and gradually became inaudible to me, until I heard only a soothing murmur, and the rattle and jar of the wheels.

Again my dreams were nervous and uneasy. I imagined I was in Cairo, threading narrow dim streets, where the camels jostled me and the black slaves threatened me, and the air was heavy with musk, and veiled faces watched me from latticed casements above. Suddenly a rose fell at my feet. I looked up, and a face like my Minnie's, only with large liquid dark eyes like an antelope's, glanced forth from behind a water-vase and smiled. At that moment, four Mamelukes appeared, riding down the street at full gallop, and came upon me with their sabres flashing. I dreamed I had only one hope, and that was to repeat the talismanic words of my letter-locks. Already I was under the hoofs of the Mamelukes' horses. I cried out with great difficulty, "Cotopaxo! Cotopaxo!" A rough shake awoke me. It was the major, looking bluff but stern.

"Why, you're talking in your sleep!" he said; "why the devil do you talk in your sleep? Bad habit. Here we are at the breakfast-place."

"What was I talking about?" I asked, with ill-concealed alarm.

"Some foreign gibberish," returned the major.

"Greek, I think," said Levison; "but I was just off too."

We reached Marseilles. I rejoiced to see its almond-trees and its white villas. I should feel safer when I was on board ship, and my treasure with me. I was not of a suspicious temperament, but I had thought it remarkable that during that long journey from Lyons to the seaboard, I had never fallen asleep without waking and finding an eye upon me—either the major's or his wife's. Levison had slept during the last four hours incessantly. Latterly, we had all of us grown silent, and even rather sullen. Now we brightened up.

"Hôtel de Londres! Hôtel de l'Univers! Hôtel Impérial!" cried the touts, as we stood round our luggage, agreeing to keep together.

"Hôtel Impérial, of course," said the major; "best house."

A one-eyed saturnine half-caste tout shrunk up to us.

"Hôtel Impérial, sare. I am Hôtel Impérial; all full; not a bed; no—pas de tout—no use, sare!"

"Hang it! the steamer will be the next thing to fail."

"Steamer, sare—accident with boiler; won't start till minuit et vingt minutes—half-past midnight, sare."

"Where shall we go?" said I, turning round and smiling at the three blank faces of my companions. "Our journey seems doomed to be unlucky. Let us redeem it by a parting supper. My telegraphing done, I am free till half-past eleven."

"I will take you," said Levison, "to a small but very decent hotel down by the harbour. The Hôtel des Etrangers."

"Cursed low nasty crib—gambling place!" said the major, lighting a cheroot, as he got into an open fly.

Mr. Levison drew himself up in his punctilious way. "Sir," he said, "the place is in new hands, or I would not have recommended the house, you may rely upon it."

"Sir," said the major, lifting his broad-brimmed white hat, "I offer you my apologies. I was not aware of that."

"My dear sir, never mention the affair again."

"Major, you're a hot-headed simpleton," were Mrs. B.'s last words, as we drove off together.

As we entered a bare-looking salou with a dinner-table in the middle and a dingy billiard-table at one end, the major said to me, "I shall go and wash and dress for the theatre, and then take a stroll while you do your telegraphing. Go up first, Julia, and see the rooms."

"What slaves we poor women are!" said Mrs. B., as she sailed out.

"And I," said Levison, laying down his rail-way rug, "shall go out and try and do some business before the shops shut. We have agents here in the Canabière."

"Only two double-bedded rooms, sare," said the one-eyed tout, who stood over the luggage.

"That will do," said Levison, promptly, and with natural irritation at our annoyances. "My friend goes by the boat to-night; he does not sleep here. His luggage can be put in my room, and he can take the key, in case he comes in first."

"Then now we are all right," said the major. "So far, so good!"

When I got to the telegraph-office, I found a telegram from London awaiting me. To my surprise and horror, it contained only these words:

"You are in great danger. Do not wait a moment on shore. There is a plot against you. Apply to the prefect for a guard."

It must be the major, and I was in his hands! That rough hearty manner of his was all a trick. Even now, he might be carrying off the chests. I telegraphed back:

"Safe at Marseilles. All right up to this."

Thinking of the utter ruin of our house if I were robbed, and of dear Minnie, I flew back to the hotel, which was situated in a dirty narrow street near the harbour. As I turned down the street, a man darted from a doorway and seized my arm. It was one of the waiters. He said hurriedly, in French: "Quick, quick, monsieur; Major Baxter is anxious to see you, instantly, in the salon. There is no time to lose."

I ran to the hotel, and darted into the salon. There was the major pacing up and down in extraordinary excitement; his wife was looking anxiously out of window. The manner of both was entirely changed. The major ran up and seized me by the hand. "I am a detective officer, and my name is Arnott," he said. "That man Levison is a notorious thief. He is at this moment in his room, opening one of your specie chests. You must help me to nab him. I knew his little game, and have check-mated him. But I wanted to catch him in the act. Julia, finish that brandy-and-water while Mr. Blamyre and myself transact our business. Have you got a revolver, Mr. Blamyre, in case he shows fight? I prefer this." (He pulled out a staff.)

"I have left my revolver in the bedroom," I breathlessly exclaimed.

"That's bad; never mind, he is not likely to hit us in the flurry. He may not even think of it. You must rush at the door at the same moment as I do. These foreign locks are never any good. It's No. 15. Gently!"

We came to the door. We listened a moment. We could hear the sound of money chinking in a bag. Then a low dry laugh, as Levison chuckled over the word he had heard me utter in my sleep. "Cotopaxo—ha! ha!"

The major gave the word, and we both rushed at the door. It shook, splintered, was driven in. Levison, revolver in hand, stood over the open box, ankle deep in gold. He had already filled a huge digger's belt that was round his waist, and a courier's bag that hung at his side. A carpet-bag, half full, lay at his feet, and, as he let it fall to open the window bolt, it gushed forth a perfect torrent of gold. He did not utter a word. There were ropes at the window, as if he had been lowering, or preparing to lower, bags into the side alley. He gave a whistle, and some vehicle could be heard to drive furiously off.

"Surrender, you gallows-bird! I know you," cried the major. "Surrender! I've got you now, old boy."

Levison's only reply was to pull the trigger of the revolver; fortunately, there was no discharge. I had forgotten to cap it.

"The infernal thing is not capped. One for you, Bobby," he said quietly. Then hurling it at the major with a sudden fury, he threw open the window and leaped out.

I leaped after him—it was a ground floor room—raising a hue and cry. Arnott remained to guard the money.

A moment more and a wild rabble of soldiers, sailors, mongrel idlers, and porters, were pursuing the flying wretch with screams and hoots, as in the dim light (the lamps were just beginning to be kindled) we tore after him, doubling and twisting like a hare, among the obstacles that crowded the quay. Hundreds of blows were aimed at him; hundreds of hands were stretched to seize him; he wrested himself from one; he felled another; he leaped over a third; a Zouave's clutch was all but on him, when suddenly his foot caught in a mooring ring, and he fell headlong into the harbour. There was a shout as he splashed and disappeared in the dark water, near which the light of only one lamp moved and glittered. I ran down the nearest steps and waited while the gendarmes took a boat and stolidly dragged with hooks for the body.

"They are foxes, these old thieves. I remember this man here at Toulon. I saw him branded. I knew his face again in a moment. He has dived under the shipping, got into some barge and hid. You'll never see him again," said an old grey gendarme who had taken me into the boat.

"Yes we shall, for here he is!" cried a second, stooping down and lifting a body out of the water by the hair.

"Oh, he *was* an artful file," said a man from a boat behind us. It was Arnott. "Just came to see how you were getting on, sir. It's all right with the money; Julia's minding it. I often said that fellow would catch it some day, now he's got it. He all but had you, Mr. Blamyre. He'd have cut your throat when you were asleep, rather than miss the money. But I was on his track. He didn't know me. This was my first cruise for some time against this sort of rogue. Well; his name is off the books; that's one good thing. Come, comrades, bring that body to land. We must strip him of the money he has upon him, which at least did one good thing while in his possession—it sent the scoundrel to the bottom."

Even in death, the long face looked craftily respectable when we turned it to the lamp-light.

Arnott told me all, in his jovial way, on my return to the hotel, where I loaded him and Mrs. B. (another officer) with thanks. On the night I started, he had received orders from the London head office to follow me, and watch Levison. He had not had time to communicate with my partners. The driver of our train had been bribed to make the engine break down at Fort Rouge, where Levison's accomplices were waiting with carts to carry off the luggage in the confusion and darkness, or even during a sham riot and fight. This plan Arnott had frustrated by getting the police to telegraph from Paris, for soldiers to be sent from Lyons, and be kept in readiness, at the station. The champagne he spilt had been drugged. Levison, defeated in his first attempt, had then resolved to try other means. My unlucky disclosure of the mystery of the letter-lock had furnished him with the power of opening that one chest. The break-down of the steamer, which was accidental (as far as could ever be ascertained), gave him a last opportunity.

That night, thanks to Arnott, I left Marseilles with not one single piece of money lost. The journey was prosperous. The loan was effected on very profitable terms. Our house has flourished ever since, and Minnie and I have flourished likewise—and increased.

VI.

TO BE TAKEN WITH A GRAIN OF SALT.

I have always noticed a prevalent want of courage, even among persons of superior intelligence and culture, as to imparting their own psychological experiences when those have been of a strange sort. Almost all men are afraid that what they could relate in such wise would find no parallel or response in a listener's internal life, and might be suspected or laughed at. A truthful traveller who should have seen some extraordinary creature in the likeness of a sea-serpent, would have no fear of mentioning it; but the same traveller having had some singular presentiment, impulse, vagary of thought, vision (so-called), dream, or other remarkable mental impression, would hesitate considerably before he would own to it. To this reticence I attribute much of the obscurity in which such subjects are involved. We do not habitually communicate our experiences of these subjective things, as we do our experiences of objective creation. The consequence is, that the general stock of experience in this regard appears exceptional, and really is so, in respect of being miserably imperfect.

In what I am going to relate I have no intention of setting up, opposing, or supporting, any theory whatever. I know the history of the Bookseller of Berlin, I have studied the case of the wife of a late Astronomer Royal as related by Sir David Brewster, and I have followed the minutest details of a much more remarkable case of Spectral Illusion occurring within my private circle of friends. It may be necessary to state as to this last that the sufferer (a lady) was in no degree, however distant, related to me. A mistaken assumption on that head, might suggest an explanation of a part of my own case—but only a part—which would be wholly without foundation. It cannot be referred to my inheritance of any developed peculiarity, nor had I ever before any at all similar experience, nor have I ever had any at all similar experience since.

It does not signify how many years ago, or how few, a certain Murder was committed in England, which attracted great attention. We hear more than enough of Murderers as they rise in succession to their atrocious eminence, and I would bury the memory of this particular brute, if I could, as his body was buried, in Newgate Jail. I purposely abstain from giving any direct clue to the criminal's individuality.

When the murder was first discovered, no suspicion fell—or I ought rather to say, for I cannot be too precise in my facts, it was nowhere publicly hinted that any suspicion fell—on the man who was afterwards brought to trial. As no reference was at that time made to him in the newspapers, it is obviously impossible that any description of him can at that time have been given in the newspapers. It is essential that this fact be remembered.

Unfolding at breakfast my morning paper, containing the account of that first discovery, I found it to be deeply interesting, and I read it with close attention. I read it twice, if not three times. The discovery had been made in a bedroom, and, when I laid down the paper, I was aware of a flash—rush—flow—I do not know what to call it—no word I can find is satisfactorily descriptive—in which I seemed to see that bedroom passing through my room, like a picture impossibly painted on a running river. Though almost instantaneous in its passing, it was perfectly clear; so clear that I distinctly, and with a sense of relief, observed the absence of the dead body from the bed.

It was in no-romantic place that I had this curious sensation, but in chambers in Piccadilly, very near to the corner of Saint James's-street. It was entirely new to me. I was in my easy-chair at the moment, and the sensation was accompanied with a peculiar shiver which started the chair from its position. (But it is to be noted that the chair ran easily on castors.) I went to one of the windows (there are two in the room, and the room is on the second floor) to refresh my eyes with the moving objects down in Piccadilly. It was a bright autumn morning, and the street was sparkling and cheerful. The wind was high. As I looked out, it brought down from the Park a quantity of fallen leaves, which a gust took, and whirled into a spiral pillar. As the pillar fell and the leaves dispersed, I saw two men on the opposite side of the way, going from West to East. They were one behind the other. The foremost man often looked back over his shoulder. The second man followed him, at a distance of some thirty paces, with his right hand menacingly raised. First, the singularity and steadiness of this threatening gesture in so public a thoroughfare, attracted my attention; and next, the more remarkable circumstance that nobody heeded it. Both men threaded their way among the other passengers, with a smoothness hardly consistent even with the action of walking on a pavement, and no single creature that I could see, gave them place, touched them, or looked after them. In passing before my windows, they both stared up at me. I saw their two faces very distinctly, and I knew that I could recognise them anywhere. Not that I had consciously noticed anything very remarkable in either face, except that the man who went first had an unusually lowering appearance, and that the face of the man who followed him was of the colour of impure wax.

I am a bachelor, and my valet and his wife constitute my whole establishment. My occupation is in a certain Branch Bank, and I wish that my duties as head of a Department were as light as they are popularly supposed to be. They kept me in town that autumn, when I stood in need of change. I was not ill, but I was not well. My reader is to make the most that can be reasonably made of my feeling jaded, having a depressing sense upon me of a monotonous life, and being "slightly dyspeptic." I am assured by my renowned doctor that my real state of health at that time justifies no stronger description, and I quote his own from his written answer to my request for it.

As the circumstances of the Murder, gradually unravelling, took stronger and stronger possession of the public mind, I kept them away from mine, by knowing as little about them as was possible in the midst of the universal excitement. But I knew that a verdict of Wilful Murder had been found against the suspected Murderer, and that he had been committed to Newgate for trial. I also knew that his trial had been postponed over one Sessions of the Central Criminal Court, on the ground of general prejudice and want of time for the preparation of the defence. I may further have known, but I believe I did not, when, or about when, the Sessions to which his trial stood postponed would come on.

My sitting-room, bedroom, and dressing-room, are all on one floor. With the last, there is no communication but through the bedroom. True, there is a door in it, once communicating with the staircase; but a part of the fitting of my bath has been—and had then been for some years—fixed across it. At the same period, and as a part of the same arrangement, the door had been nailed up and canvased over.

I was standing in my bedroom late one night, giving some directions to my servant before he went to bed. My face was towards the only available door of communication with the dressing-room, and it was closed. My servant's back was towards that door. While I was speaking to him I saw it open, and a man look in, who very earnestly and mysteriously beckoned to me. That man was the man who had gone second of the two along Piccadilly, and whose face was of the colour of impure wax.

The figure, having beckoned, drew back and closed the door. With no longer pause than was made by my crossing the bedroom, I opened the dressing-room door, and looked in. I had a lighted candle already in my hand. I felt no inward expectation of seeing the figure in the dressing-room, and I did not see it there.

Conscious that my servant stood amazed, I turned round to him, and said : " Derrick, could you believe that in my cool senses I fancied I saw a——" As I there laid my hand upon his breast, with a sudden start he trembled violently, and said, "O Lord yes, sir ! A dead man beckoning !"

Now, I do not believe that this John Derrick, my trusty and attached servant for more than twenty years, had any impression whatever of having seen any such figure, until I touched him. The change in him was so startling when I touched him, that I fully believe he derived his impression in some occult manner from me at that instant.

I bade John Derrick bring some brandy, and I gave him a dram, and was glad to take one myself. Of what preceded that night's phenomenon, I told him not a single word. Reflecting on it, I was absolutely certain that I had never seen that face before, except on the one occasion in Piccadilly. Comparing its expression when beckoning at the door, with its expression when it had stared up at me as I stood at my window, I came to the conclusion that on the first occasion it had sought to fasten itself upon my memory, and that on the second occasion it had made sure of being immediately remembered.

I was not very comfortable that night, though I felt a certainty, difficult to explain, that the figure would not return. At daylight, I fell into a heavy sleep, from which I was awakened by John Derrick's coming to my bedside with a paper in his hand.

This paper, it appeared, had been the subject of an altercation at the door between its bearer and my servant. It was a summons to me to serve upon a Jury at the forthcoming Sessions of the Central Criminal Court at the Old Bailey. I had never before been summoned on such a Jury, as John Derrick well knew. He believed —I am not certain at this hour whether with reason or otherwise—that that class of Jurors were customarily chosen on a lower qualification than mine, and he had at first refused to accept the summons. The man who served it had taken the matter very coolly. He had said that my attendance or non-attendance was nothing to him; there the summons was; and I should deal with it at my own peril, and not at his.

For a day or two I was undecided whether to respond to this call, or take no notice of it. I was not conscious of the slightest mysterious bias, influence, or attraction, one way or other. Of that I am as strictly sure as of every other statement that I make here. Ultimately I decided, as a break in the monotony of my life, that I would go.

The appointed morning was a raw morning in the month of November. There was a dense brown fog in Piccadilly, and it became positively black and in the last degree oppressive East of Temple Bar. I found the passages and staircases of the Court House flaringly lighted with gas, and the Court itself similarly illuminated. I think that until I was conducted by officers into the Old Court and saw its crowded state, I did not know that the Murderer was to be tried that day. I think that until I was so helped into the Old Court with considerable difficulty, I did not know into which of the two Courts sitting, my summons would take me. But this must not be received as a positive assertion, for I am not completely satisfied in my mind on either point.

I took my seat in the place appropriated to Jurors in waiting, and I looked about the Court as well as I could through the cloud of fog and breath that was heavy in it. I noticed the black vapour hanging like a murky curtain outside the great windows, and I noticed the stifled sound of wheels on the straw or tan that was littered in the street; also, the hum of the people gathered there, which a shrill whistle, or a louder song or hail than the rest, occasionally pierced. Soon afterwards the Judges, two in number, entered and took their seats. The buzz in the Court was awfully hushed. The direction was given to put the Murderer to the bar. He appeared there. And in that same instant I recognised in him, the first of the two men who had gone down Piccadilly.

If my name had been called then, I doubt if I could have answered to it audibly. But it was called about sixth or eighth in the panel, and I was by that time able to say " Here !" Now, observe. As I stepped into the box, the prisoner, who had been looking on attentively but with no sign of concern, became violently agitated, and beckoned to his attorney. The prisoner's wish to challenge me was so manifest, that it occasioned a pause, during which the attorney, with his hand upon the dock, whispered with his client, and shook his head. I afterwards had it from that gentleman, that the prisoner's first affrighted words to him were, "*At all hazards challenge that man!*" But, that as he would give no reason for it, and admitted that he had not even known my name until he heard it called and I appeared, it was not done.

Both on the ground already explained, that I wish to avoid reviving the unwholesome memory of that Murderer, and also because a detailed account of his long trial is by no means indispensable to my narrative, I shall confine myself closely to such incidents in the ten days and nights during which we, the Jury, were kept together, as directly bear on my own curious personal experience. It is in that, and not in the Murderer, that I seek to interest my reader. It is to that, and not to a page of the Newgate Calendar, that I beg attention.

I was chosen Foreman of the Jury. On the second morning of the trial, after evidence had been taken for two hours (I heard the church clocks strike), happening to cast my eyes over my brother-jurymen, I found an inexplicable difficulty in counting them. I counted them several times, yet always with the same difficulty. In short, I made them one too many.

I touched the brother-juryman whose place was next me, and I whispered to him, "Oblige me by counting us." He looked surprised by the request, but turned his head and counted. "Why," says he, suddenly, "we are Thirt——; but no, it's not possible. No. We are twelve."

According to my counting that day, we were always right in detail, but in the gross we were always one too many. There was no appearance—no figure—to account for it; but I had now an inward foreshadowing of the figure that was surely coming.

The Jury were housed at the London Tavern. We all slept in one large room on separate tables, and we were constantly in the charge and under the eye of the officer sworn to hold us in safe-keeping. I see no reason for suppressing the real name of that officer. He was intelligent, highly polite, and obliging, and (I was glad to hear) much respected in the City. He had an agreeable presence, good eyes, enviable black whiskers, and a fine sonorous voice. His name was Mr. Harker.

When we turned into our twelve beds at night, Mr. Harker's bed was drawn across the door. On the night of the second day, not being disposed to lie down, and seeing Mr. Harker sitting on his bed, I went and sat beside him, and offered him a pinch of snuff. As Mr. Harker's hand touched mine in taking it from my box, a peculiar shiver crossed him, and he said: "Who is this!"

Following Mr. Harker's eyes and looking along the room, I saw again the figure I expected—the second of the two men who had gone down Piccadilly. I rose, and advanced a few steps; then stopped, and looked round at Mr. Harker. He was quite unconcerned, laughed, and said in a pleasant way, "I thought for a moment we had a thirteenth juryman, without a bed. But I see it is the moonlight."

Making no revelation to Mr. Harker, but inviting him to take a walk with me to the end of the room, I watched what the figure did. It stood for a few moments by the bedside of each of my eleven brother-jurymen, close to the pillow. It always went to the right-hand side of the bed, and always passed out crossing the foot of the next bed. It seemed from the action of the head, merely to look down pensively at each recumbent figure. It took no notice of me, or of my bed, which was that nearest to Mr. Harker's. It seemed to go out where the moonlight came in, through a high window, as by an aërial flight of stairs.

Next morning at breakfast, it appeared that everybody present had dreamed of the murdered man last night, except myself and Mr. Harker.

I now felt as convinced that the second man who had gone down Piccadilly was the murdered man (so to speak), as if it had been borne into my comprehension by his immediate testimony. But even this took place, and in a manner for which I was not at all prepared.

On the fifth day of the trial, when the case for the prosecution was drawing to a close, a miniature of the murdered man, missing from his bedroom upon the discovery of the deed, and afterwards found in a hiding-place where the Murderer had been seen digging, was put in evidence. Having been identified by the witness under examination, it was handed up to the Bench, and thence handed down to be inspected by the Jury. As an officer in a black gown was making his way with it across to me, the figure of the second man who had gone down Piccadilly, impetuously started from the crowd, caught the miniature from the officer, and gave it to me with its own hands, at the same time saying in a low and hollow tone—before I saw the miniature, which was in a locket—"*I was younger then, and my face was not then drained of blood.*" It also came between me and the brother juryman to whom I would have given the miniature, and between him and the brother juryman to whom he would have given it, and so passed it on through the whole of our number, and back into my possession. Not one of them, however, detected this.

At table, and generally when we were shut up together in Mr. Harker's custody, we had from the first naturally discussed the day's proceedings a good deal. On that fifth day, the case for the prosecution being closed, and we having that side of the question in a completed shape before us, our discussion was more animated and serious. Among our number was a vestryman—the densest idiot I have ever seen at large—who met the plainest evidence with the most preposterous objections, and who was sided with by two flabby parochial parasites; all the three empanelled from a district so delivered over to Fever that they ought to have been upon their own trial, for five hundred Murders. When these mischievous blockheads were at their loudest, which was towards midnight while some of us were already preparing for bed, I again saw the murdered man. He stood grimly behind them, beckoning to me. On my going towards them and striking into the conversation, he immediately retired. This was the beginning of a separate series of appearances, confined to that long room in which *we* were confined. Whenever a knot of my brother jurymen laid their heads together, I saw the head of the murdered man among theirs. Whenever their comparison of notes was going against him, he would solemnly and irresistibly beckon to me.

It will be borne in mind that down to the production of the miniature on the fifth day of the trial, I had never seen the Appearance in Court. Three changes occurred, now that we entered on the case for the defence. Two of them I will mention together, first. The figure was now in Court continually, and it never there addressed itself to me, but always to the person who was speaking at the time. For instance. The throat of the murdered man had been cut straight across. In the opening speech for the defence, it was suggested that the deceased might have cut his own throat. At that very moment, the figure with its throat in the dreadful condition referred to (this it had concealed before) stood at the speaker's elbow, motioning across and across its windpipe, now with the right hand, now with the left, vigorously suggesting to the speaker himself, the impossibility of such a wound having been self-inflicted by either hand. For another instance. A witness to character, a woman, deposed to the prisoner's being the most amiable of mankind. The figure at that instant stood on the floor before her, looking her full in the face, and pointing out the prisoner's evil countenance with an extended arm and an outstretched finger.

The third change now to be added, impressed me strongly, as the most marked and striking of all. I do not theorise upon it; I accurately state it, and there leave it. Although the Appearance was not itself perceived by those whom it addressed, its coming close to such persons was invariably attended by some trepidation or disturbance on their part. It seemed to me as if it were prevented by laws to which I was not amenable, from fully revealing itself to others, and yet as if it could, invisibly, dumbly and darkly, overshadow their minds. When the leading counsel for the defence suggested that hypothesis of suicide and the figure stood at the learned gentleman's elbow, frightfully sawing at its severed throat, it is undeniable that the counsel faltered in his speech, lost for a few seconds the thread of his ingenious discourse, wiped his forehead with his handkerchief, and turned extremely pale. When the witness to character was confronted by the Appearance, her eyes most certainly did follow the direction of its pointed finger, and rest in great hesitation and trouble upon the prisoner's face. Two additional illustrations will suffice. On the eighth day of the trial, after the pause which was every day made early in the afternoon for a few minutes' rest and refreshment, I came back into Court with the rest of the Jury, some little time before the return of the Judges. Standing up in the box and looking about me, I thought the figure was not there, until, chancing to raise my eyes to the gallery, I saw it bending forward and leaning over a very decent woman, as if to assure itself whether the Judges had resumed their seats or not. Immediately afterwards, that woman screamed, fainted, and was carried out. So with the venerable, sagacious, and patient Judge who conducted the trial. When the case was over, and he settled himself and his papers to sum up, the murdered man entering by the Judges' door, advanced to his Lordship's desk, and looked eagerly over his shoulder at the pages of his notes which he was turning. A change came over his Lordship's face; his hand stopped; the peculiar shiver that I knew so well, passed over him;

he faltered, "Excuse me, gentlemen, for a few moments. I am somewhat oppressed by the vitiated air;" and did not recover until he had drunk a glass of water.

Through all the monotony of six of those interminable ten days—the same Judges and others on the bench, the same Murderer in the dock, the same lawyers at the table, the same tones of question and answer rising to the roof of the court, the same scratching of the Judge's pen, the same ushers going in and out, the same lights kindled at the same hour when there had been any natural light of day, the same foggy curtain outside the great windows when it was foggy, the same rain pattering and dripping when it was rainy, the same footmarks of turnkeys and prisoner day after day on the same sawdust, the same keys locking and unlocking the same heavy doors—through all the wearisome monotony which made me feel as if I had been Foreman of the Jury for a vast period of time, and Piccadilly had flourished coevally with Babylon, the murdered man never lost one trace of his distinctness in my eyes, nor was he at any moment less distinct than anybody else. I must not omit, as a matter of fact, that I never once saw the Appearance which I call by the name of the murdered man, look at the Murderer. Again and again I wondered, "Why does he not?" But he never did.

Nor did he look at me, after the production of the miniature, until the last closing minutes of the trial arrived. We retired to consider, at seven minutes before ten at night. The idiotic vestryman and his two parochial parasites gave us so much trouble, that we twice returned into Court, to beg to have certain extracts from the Judge's notes re-read. Nine of us had not the smallest doubt about those passages, neither, I believe, had any one in Court; the dunderheaded triumvirate however, having no idea but obstruction, disputed them for that very reason. At length we prevailed, and finally the Jury returned into Court at ten minutes past twelve.

The murdered man at that time stood directly opposite the Jury-box, on the other side of the Court. As I took my place, his eyes rested on me, with great attention; he seemed satisfied, and slowly shook a great grey veil, which he carried on his arm for the first time, over his head and whole form. As I gave in our verdict "Guilty," the veil collapsed, all was gone, and his place was empty.

The Murderer being asked by the Judge, according to usage, whether he had anything to say before sentence of Death should be passed upon him, indistinctly muttered something which was described in the leading newspapers of the following day as "a few rambling, incoherent, and half-audible words, in which he was understood to complain that he had not had a fair trial, because the Foreman of the Jury was prepossessed against him." The remarkable declaration that he really made, was this: " *My Lord, I knew I was a doomed man when the Foreman of my Jury came into the box. My Lord, I knew he would*

never let me off, because, before I was taken, he
somehow got to my bedside in the night, woke me,
and put a rope round my neck."

VII.

TO BE TAKEN AND TRIED.

There can hardly be seen anywhere, a prettier village than Cumner, standing on the brow of a hill which commands one of the finest views in England, and flanked by its broad breezy common, the air of which is notorious for clearness and salubrity. The high road from Dring, for the most part shut in by the fences of gentlemen's seats, opens out when it reaches this common, and, separating from the Tenelms road, ascends in a north-westerly direction till it comes in sight of Cumner. Every step is against the collar, yet so gradual is the ascent, that you scarcely realise it until, turning, you behold the magnificent panorama spread around and beneath.

The village consists chiefly of one short street of somewhat straggling houses, among which you observe its little post-office, its police station, its rustic public-house (the Dunstan Arms), whose landlord also holds the general shop across the way; and its two or three humble lodging-houses. Facing you as you enter the street, which is a cul-de-sac, is the quaint old church, standing not more than a bow-shot from the Rectory. There is something primitive and almost patriarchal in this quiet village, where the pastor lives surrounded by his flock, and can scarcely move from his own gate without finding himself in the midst of them.

Cumner Common is skirted on three sides by dwellings, varying in size and importance, from the small butcher's shop standing in its own garden, and under the shadow of its own apple-trees, to the pretty white house where the curate lodges, and the more pretentious abodes of those who are, or consider themselves, gentry. It is bounded on the east by the low stone wall and gateway of Mr. Malcolmson's domain; the modest dwelling of Simon Eade, that gentleman's bailiff, half covered with creepers, the autumnal hues of which might rival the brightest specimens of American foliage; lastly, by the high brick wall (with its door in the centre), which completely shuts in Mr. Gibbs's "place." On the south side runs the high road to Tenelms, skirting the great Southanger property, of which Sir Oswald Dunstan is proprietor.

Hardly could the pedestrian tourist, on his way from Dring, fail to pause at the rustic stile nearly opposite the blacksmith's forge, and, resting upon it, gaze down on the magnificent prospect of wood and water spread at his feet—a prospect to which two ancient cedars form no inappropriate foreground. That stile is not often crossed, for the footpath from it leads only to the farm called the Plashetts; but it is very constantly used as a resting-place. Many an artist has sketched the view from it; many a lover has whispered tender words to his mistress beside it; many a weary tramp has rested his or her feet on the worn stone beneath.

This stile was once the favourite resort of two young lovers, inhabitants of the district, and soon to be united. George Eade, the only son of Mr. Malcolmson's bailiff, was a stalwart good-looking young fellow of some six-and-twenty, who worked for that gentleman under his father, and was in the receipt of liberal wages. Honest, steady, and fond of self-cultivation, he was capable, if not clever —persevering, if not rapid—an excellent specimen of an honest English peasant. But he had certain peculiarities of disposition and temper, which served to render him considerably less popular than his father. He was reserved; feeling strongly, but with difficulty giving expression to his feelings; susceptible to, and not easily forgiving, injuries; singularly addicted to self-accusation and remorse. His father, a straightforward open-hearted man of five-and-forty, who had raised himself by sheer merit from the position of a labourer to that of the trusted manager of Mr. Malcolmson's property, was highly respected by that gentleman, and by the whole country-side. His mother, feeble in health, but energetic of spirit, was one of the most excellent of women.

This couple, like many of their class, had married imprudently early, and had struggled through many difficulties in consequence: burying, one after another, three sickly children in the little churchyard at Cumner where they hoped one day themselves to lie. On the one son that remained to them their affections were centred. The mother, especially, worshipped her George with an admiring love that partook of idolatry. She was not without some of the weaknesses of her sex. She was jealous; and when she discovered the flame which had been kindled in the heart of her son by the soft blue eyes of Susan Archer, her feelings towards that rosy-cheeked damsel were not those of perfect charity. True, the Archers were people who held themselves high, occupying a large farm under Sir Oswald Dunstan; and they were known to regard Susan's attachment as a decided lowering of herself and them. That attachment had sprung up, as is not un frequently the case, in the hop-gardens. The girl had been ailing for some time, and her shrewd old doctor assured her father that there was no tonic so efficacious as a fortnight's hop-picking in the sunny September weather. Now there were but few places to which so distinguished a belle as Susan could be permitted to go for such a purpose; but her family knew and respected the Eades, and to Mr. Malcolmson's hop-grounds she was accordingly sent. The tonic prescribed produced the desired effect. She lost her ailments; but she lost her heart too.

George Eade was good looking, and up to that time had never cared for woman. The love he conceived for the gentle, blue-eyed girl was of that all-absorbing character which natures stern and concentrated like his, are fitted to feel, and to feel but once in a lifetime. It carried all before it. Susan was sweet tempered and simple hearted, of a yielding disposition, and, though not unconscious of her beauty, singularly little spoilt by the consciousness. She gave her whole heart to the faithful earnest man whom she reverenced as her superior in moral strength, if not in outward circumstances. They exchanged no rings on the balmy evening which witnessed their plighted faith, but he took from her hat the garland of hops she had laughingly twisted round it, and looking down upon her sweet face with a great love in his brown eyes, whispered, "I shall keep this whilst I live, and have it buried with me when I die!"

But, there was a certain Geoffrey Gibbs, the owner of the "Place" on Cumner Common, who had paid, and was still paying, marked attention to the beautiful Susan. This man, originally in trade, had chanced, some years before, to see in the newspapers a notice that if he would apply to a certain lawyer in London, he would hear of something greatly to his advantage. He did so, and the result was, his acquisition of a comfortable independence, left him by a distant kinsman whom he had never so much as seen. This windfall changed his whole prospects and manner of life, but not his character, which had always been that of an unmitigated snob. In outward circumstances, however, he was a gentleman living on his income, and, as such, the undoubted social superior of the Archers, who were simply tenant-farmers. Hence their desire that Susan should favour his suit. Some people were of opinion, that he had no serious intention of marrying the girl; and Susan herself always encouraged this notion; adding, that were he ten times as rich, and a hundred times as devoted as he represented himself to be, she would die rather than accept the cross-grained monster.

He *was* frightful; less from defects of feature than from utter disproportion of form, and a sinister expression of countenance, far worse than actual ugliness. His legs were as short as his body and hands were long, while his head would have been well suited to the frame of a Hercules; giving him a top-heavy appearance that was singularly ungraceful. His eyebrows were shaggy and overhanging, his eyes small and malicious looking, his nose was beak-shaped, his mouth immense, with thick sensual lips. He wore huge false-looking chains, outrageous shirt-pins and neckcloths, and cutaway sporting coats of astounding colours. He was a man who delighted in frightening inoffensive females, in driving within an inch of a lady's pony-carriage, or in violently galloping past some timid girl on horseback, and chuckling at her scared attempts to restrain her plunging steed. Like all bullies, he was of course a coward at heart.

Between this man and George Eade a keen hatred existed. George despised as well as detested Gibbs. Gibbs envied as much as he abhorred the more fortunate peasant, who was beloved where he met with nothing but coldness and rebuffs.

Susan's heart was indeed wholly George's, yet it was only when her health had again begun to fail, that her father was frightened into a most unwilling consent to their union; which consent no sooner became known to Mr. Malcolmson, than he voluntarily raised the young man's wages, and undertook to put in repair for him a cottage of his own, not far from that of Simon Eade.

But, when the news of the approaching marriage reached the ears of Gibbs, his jealous fury was aroused to the utmost. He rushed down to the Plashetts, and, closeting himself with Mr. Archer, made brilliant offers of settlement on Susan, if she would consent even now to throw over her lover, and become his wife. But he only succeeded in distressing the girl, and tantalising her father. Willingly, indeed, would the latter have acceded to his wishes, but he had passed his solemn word to George, and Susan held him to it. No sooner, however, was Gibbs gone, than the old man burst into loud lamentations over what he called her self-sacrifice; and her eldest brother coming in, joined in reproaching her for refusing prospects so advantageous. Susan was weak, and easily influenced. She was cut to the heart by their cruel words, and went out to meet her lover with her spirits depressed, and her eyes red and swollen. George, shocked at her appearance, listened with indignation to her agitated recital of what had passed.

"Keep your carriage, indeed!" he exclaimed, with bitter scorn. "Does your father make more count of a one-horse shay than of true love such as mine? And a fellow like Gibbs, too! That I wouldn't trust a dog with!"

"Father don't see it so," the girl sobbed out. "Father says he'd make a very good husband, once we was married. And I'd be a lady, and dress fine, and have servants! Father thinks so much of that!"

"So it seems; but don't you be led by him, Susan, darling! 'Tisn't riches and fine clothes that makes folks' happiness—'tis better things! See here, my girl——" He stopped short, and faced her with a look of unutterable emotion. "I love ye so true, that if I thought—if I thought it'd be for your good to marry this fellow—if I thought ye'd be happier with him than with me, I'd—I'd give ye up, Susan! Yes—and never come near ye more! I would indeed!"

He paused, and, raising his hand with a gesture that had in it a rude solemnity very impressive, repeated once more, "I *would indeed!* But ye'd not be happy with Geoffrey Gibbs. Ye'd be miserable—ill-used, perhaps. He ain't a man to make any woman happy—I'm as sure o' that, as that I stand here. He's bad at heart—downright cruel. And I!—what I promise, I'll act up to—O! steady. I'll work for you, and slave for you, and—and love you true!"

He drew her towards him as he spoke, and she, reassured by his words, nestled lovingly to his side. And so they walked on for some moments in silence.

"And, darling," he added, presently; "I've that trust—that faith—in me—that once we're married, and you're mine—safe—so's no one can come between us, I'll get on; and who knows but ye may ride in your carriage yet. Folks do get on, when they've a mind to, serious."

She looked up at him with fond admiring eyes. She honoured him for his strength, all the more because of her own weakness.

"I don't want no carriage," she murmured; "I want nothing but you, George. 'Tisn't I, you know, that wish things different—'tis father——"

The moon had risen, the beautiful bright September moon, nearly at the full; and its light shone on the lovers as they retraced their steps through the silent Southanger woods—how solemn and lovely at that hour!—towards Susan's home. And before they had reached the gate of the Plashetts, her sweet face was again bright with smiles, and it had been agreed between them that to avoid a repetition of such attempts on the part of Gibbs, and such scenes with her father, she should propose to go to her aunt's, Miss Jane Archer's, at Ormiston, for a fortnight of the three weeks that yet remained before the marriage should take place.

She acted on this idea, and George took advantage of her absence to attend a sale on the other side of the county, and procure certain articles of furniture required for their new home. Once away, he obtained leave to prolong his stay with a friend till the time of Susan's return. It was pleasanter for him not to be at home at this period. His mother seemed to grow more averse to his marriage, the nearer it approached; declaring that no good could possibly come of union with a girl who had been too much waited upon and flattered, to make a good wife for a plain hard-working man. These remarks, indescribably galling to the lover because not wholly without foundation, had given rise to more than one dispute between his mother and him, which had not tended to diminish the half-unconscious dislike the good woman felt towards her future daughter-in-law.

When George returned home after his fortnight's holiday, he found, instead of the expected letter from his betrothed announcing her arrival at the Plashetts, one addressed to him in a strange hand, and containing the following words:

"George Eade, you are being done. Look to G. G.

"A WELL-WISHER."

Perplexed at so mysterious a communication, he was somewhat annoyed to find that Gibbs had quitted Cumner from the very day after his own departure, and was still absent. This struck him as remarkable; but Susan had written him only a week before, a letter so full of tenderness that he could not bring himself to entertain a single doubt of her truth. But on the very next morning, his mother handed him a letter from Farmer Archer, enclosing one from his sister, informing him that her niece had left her house clandestinely two days before, to be married to Mr. Gibbs. It appeared that the girl had gone, as on previous occasions, to spend the day with a cousin, and that not re-

turning at night, it was concluded she had settled to sleep there. The next morning had brought, instead of herself, the announcement of her marriage.

On reading this news, George was at first conscious of but one feeling. Utter incredulity. There must be some error somewhere; the thing could not be. While his father, with tears in his honest eyes, exhorted him to bear up like a man under this blow, and his mother indignantly declared that a girl who could so conduct herself was indeed a good riddance, he sat silent, half stupified. Such a breach of faith seemed, to his earnest and loyal nature, simply impossible.

Another half-hour brought confirmation that could not be doubted. James Wilkins, Mr. Gibbs's man-servant, came grinning and important, with a letter for George, which had been enclosed in one from his master to himself. It was from Susan, and signed with her new name.

"I know," it said, "that for what I have done, I shall be without excuse in your eyes—that you will hate and despise me as much as you have hitherto loved and trusted me. I know that I have behaved to you very, very bad, and I don't ask you to forgive me. I know you can't. But I do ask you to refrain from vengeance. It can't bring back the past. Oh, George! if ever you cared for me, listen to what I entreat now. Hate and despise me—I don't expect no other —but don't you revenge my ill conduct on anyone. Forget all about me—that's the best thing for both of us. It would have been better if we had never beheld one another."

Much more followed in the same strain—weak, self-accusing, fearful of consequences—wholly unworthy of George.

He gazed at the letter, holding it in those strong sinewy hands that would have toiled for her so hard and so faithfully. Then, without a word, he held it out to his father, and left the room. They heard him mount the narrow stairs, lock himself into his little garret, and they heard no more.

After a while his mother went to him. Although personally relieved at her son's release, that feeling was entirely absorbed in tender and loving pity for what she knew must be his sufferings. He was sitting by the little casement, a withered branch of hops upon his knee. She went and laid her cheek to his.

"Have patience, lad!" she said, with earnest feeling. "Try—try—to have faith, and comfort'll be sent ye in time. It's hard to bear, I know—dreadful hard and bitter—but for the poor parents' sakes who loves ye so dear, try and bear it."

He looked up at her with cold tearless eyes. "I will," he said, in a hard voice. "Don't ye see I am trying?"

His glance was dull and hopeless. How she longed that tears would come and relieve his bursting heart!

"She wasn't worthy of ye, my boy. I always told ye——"

But he stopped her with a stern gesture.

"Mother! Not a word o' that, nor of her, from this hour. What she's done ain't so very bad after all. *I'm* all right—*I* am. Father and you shan't see no difference in me, leastways, not if you'll forbear naming of her ever, ever again. She's turned my heart to stone, that's all! No great matter!"

He laid his hand on his broad chest and heaved a great gasping sigh. "This morning I had a heart o' flesh here," he said; "now it's a cold, heavy stone. But it's no great matter."

"Oh, don't ye speak like that, my lad!" his mother cried, bursting into tears, and throwing her arms around him. "It kills me to hear ye!"

But he gently unwound those arms, and kissing her on the cheek, led her to the door. "I must go to work now," he said; and, descending the stairs before her, he quitted the cottage with a firm step.

From that hour no one heard him speak of Susan Gibbs. He never inquired into the circumstances of her stay at Ormiston; he never spoke of them, nor of her, to her relations or to his own. He avoided the former; he was silent and reserved with the latter. Susan appeared to be, for him, as though she had never been.

And from that hour he was an altered being. He went about his work as actively, and did it as carefully, as ever; but it was done sternly, doggedly, like an imperative but unwelcome duty. No man ever saw a smile upon his lips; no jocular word ever escaped them. Grave and uncompromising, he went his ungenial way, seeking for no sympathy, and bestowing none, avoiding all companionship save that of his parents;—a sad and solitary man.

Meanwhile, Mr. Gibbs's "Place" on Cumner Common was advertised as to be let; strangers hired it, and for nearly three years nothing was seen of him or of his wife. Then news arrived one day that they were to be expected shortly, and quite a ferment of expectation was created in the little village. They came, and certain rumours that had reached it from time to time were found to have only too much foundation in truth.

For it had oozed out, as such things do ooze, that Gibbs shamefully ill used his pretty wife, and that the marriage, which on his side had been one of love, had turned out miserably. Her father and brothers, who had been to see them more than once, had been strangely reserved on the subject of those visits, and it was generally understood that the old farmer lamented his daughter's marriage now, as much as he had formerly longed for it. No one wondered, when they saw her. She was the shadow of her former self; still lovely, but broken, cowed, pale; all the bloom faded; all the spirit crushed out of her. No smile was ever seen upon those pretty lips now, except when she played with her boy, a fair-haired little fellow, the image of herself. But even in her intercourse with this child she was sternly restricted, and her tyrant would not unfrequently dismiss him with an oath, and forbid her to follow him to his nursery.

In spite of their being such near neighbours, the Gibbses had been some time in the place before George met his former love. He never went to Cumner church (nor to any, indeed),

and she never quitted her own house, except to drive with her husband, or walk through the Southanger Woods to her father's. George might have beheld her driving past his father's door with a high-stepping horse that always seemed on the point of running away; but he never looked at her, nor replied to his mother's remarks respecting her and her smart turn-out. Yet though he resolutely kept the door of his own lips, he could not close the lips of other people, or his own ears. Do what he would, the Gibbses and their doings pursued him still. His master's labourers gossiped about the husband's brutality; the baker's boy had no end of stories to tell, of the oaths he had heard, and even the blows he had witnessed, when "Gibbs was more than usual excited with drink." The poor frightened wife was understood to have declared that but for her dread of what he might be driven to do in his fury, she would go before a magistrate and swear the peace against him. George could not close his ears to all this; and men said that the expression of his eyes on those occasions was not good to look upon.

One Sunday, the Eades were sitting over their frugal one o'clock dinner, when they heard the sound of a carriage driving furiously past. Mrs. Eade caught up her stick, and, in spite of her lameness, hobbled to the window. "I thought so!" she cried. "It's Gibbs driving to Tenelms, and drunk again, seemingly. See how he's flogging of the horse. And he's got the little lad, too! He'll not rest till he've broken that child's neck, or the mother's. Simmons declares——"

She stopped, suddenly aware of her son's breath upon her cheek. He had actually come to the window, and now, leaning over her, was gazing sternly at the figures in the carriage, flying down the hill towards the Tenelms road. "I wish he might break his own neck!" George muttered between his teeth.

"Oh, George! George! don't name such things," Mrs. Eade cried, with a pale shocked face. "It ain't Christian. We've all need of repentance, and our times is in His hand."

"If ye frequented church, my lad, 'stead of keeping away, as I grieve to see ye do," his father said, severely, "ye'd have better feelings in your heart. *They'll* never prosper ye, mark my words."

George had returned to his seat, but he rose again as his father said this. "Church!" he cried, in a loud harsh voice—"I was going there once, and it wasn't permitted. I'll go there no more. D'ye think," he continued, while his white lips trembled with uncontrollable emotion—" d'ye think, because I'm quiet, and do my work reg'lar, d'ye think I've forgotten? *Forgotten!*" He brought his clenched fist down upon the table with startling violence. "I tell ye when I forget, I'll be lying stark and stiff in my coffin! Let be—let be!" as his mother tried to interrupt him; "ye mean well, I know, but women haven't the judgment to tell when to speak, and when to hold hard. Ye'd best never name that scoundrel 'fore me again, nor yet church." With that, he went from the room and from the house,

Mrs. Eade fretted sadly over these evidences of George's rancorous and ungodly disposition. To her, he seemed to be on the high road to perdition, and she ended by sending to Mr. Murray, the rector, to beg he would be pleased to look in upon her some morning soon, as she was greatly troubled in her mind. But Mr. Murray was at that time ill, and nearly a fortnight elapsed before he was able to answer her summons. Meanwhile, other events occurred.

It was notorious that one of Mrs. Gibbs's greatest trials was about her boy, whom her husband persisted in driving out, at the risk, as every one thought, of his life. Fearful had been the scenes between the parents on this account; but the more she wept and implored, the more he resisted her entreaties. One day, to frighten her still more, he placed the little fellow, with the whip in his hand, on the carriage-seat alone, and stood at his door himself, loosely holding the reins, and jeering at his wife, who in an agony of terror kept beseeching him to get in, or to let her do so. Suddenly the report of a gun was heard in a neighbouring field; the horse took fright, and started off wildly, jerking the reins from the hands of the half-intoxicated Gibbs; the whip fell from the hands of the child on the animal's back, still further exciting it; and the boy, thrown with violence to the bottom of the carriage, lay half stunned by the shock.

George was close by when this occurred. He threw himself on the flying horse, and, seizing the bearing-rein with his whole strength, held on like grim death, in spite of being half dragged, half borne, along in its headlong flight. At last the animal, getting its legs entangled in the long trailing reins, fell with fearful violence, and lay stunned and motionless. George was thrown to the ground, but escaped with a few trifling bruises. The child at the bottom of the carriage, though frightened and screaming, was altogether uninjured. In less than five minutes half the village was collected on the spot, inquiring, congratulating, applauding; and Susan, with her rescued child clinging to her bosom, was covering George's hands with passionate tears and kisses.

"Bless you! Bless you a thousand times!" she cried, sobbing hysterically. "You've saved my darling's life! He might have been killed but for you! How can I ever——"

But a rough hand shoved her aside. "What are you after now?" Gibbs's furious voice was heard to cry, with a shocking oath. "Leave that fellow alone, or I'll——! Are you making a fool of yourself this way, because he's lamed the horse so that he'll have to be shot?"

The poor thing sank down on the bank and broke into a fit of hysterical weeping; whilst a murmur of "Shame, shame!" rose among the bystanders.

George Eade had turned coldly from Susan when she rushed up to him, and had striven to withdraw his hands from her grasp; but now, confronting Gibbs, he said, "It'll be a good deed done, whoever shoots that brute of yours, and it'd be a better still to shoot you as a man would a mad dog!"

All heard the words. All trembled at his look as he uttered them. The whole of the pent-up rage and resentment of the last three years seemed concentrated in that one look of savage and unutterable hatred.

Mr. Murray found poor Mrs. Eade very suffering, when, two mornings after, he called to congratulate her on her son's escape. She had not closed her eyes since the accident. George's look and words, as they had been described to her, haunted her. The good clergyman could give her but scant comfort. He had tried again and again to reason with and soften her son, but ineffectually. George answered him, with a certain rude respect, that as long as he did his work properly, and injured no man, he had a right to decide for himself in matters concerning only himself; and one of his fixed decisions was never again to see the inside of a church.

"It's a hard trial, my good friend," said Mr. Murray, "a hard and mysterious trial. But I say to you, have faith. There is a hidden good in it, that we can't see now."

"It'd be strange if I wasn't thankful for his being spared," Mrs. Eade replied. "It'd be worse than anything to have the dear lad took, revengeful and unforgiving as he is now. But you see, sir——"

She was stopped in her eager speech by a knock at the door. The son of Mr. Beach, the neighbouring butcher, peeped in. He scraped a bow on seeing the clergyman sitting with her, and looked from one to the other with a doubtful demeanour.

"I don't want nothing this morning, thank you, Jim," Mrs. Eade said. Then, struck with the peculiar expression of the young man's face, she added: "Ain't Mr. Beach so well this morning? You look all nohow."

"I'm—I'm a bit flustered," the youth replied, wiping his steaming forehead; "I've just been seeing him, and it gave me such a turn!"

"Him! who?"

"Sure! Haven't ye heard, sir? Gibbs have been found dead in Southanger Woods—murdered last night. They say——"

"Gibbs murdered!"

There was a pause of breathless horror.

"They've been carrying his corpse to the Dunstan Arms, and I see it."

Mrs. Eade turned so deadly faint that the clergyman called out hurriedly for Jemima, the servant girl. But Jemima had run out wildly on hearing the appalling intelligence, and was now midway between her master's house and the Gibbs's, listening to a knot of people, all wondering, surmising, gazing with scared eyes at that door in the high wall, the threshold of which its master would never cross again, except feet foremost.

The Eades' parlour was soon full to overflowing. Most of the dwellers on the common had congregated there—why, perhaps none would have cared to explain. Simon Eade came in among the first, and was doing his best to soothe and restore the poor fainting woman, who could hardly as yet realise what had occurred. In the midst of the confusion—the questioning, the describing of the position of the body, the rifled pockets, the dreadful blow from behind, the number of hours since the deed was done—in the midst of all this, steps were heard outside, and George came into the midst of them.

Then a sudden hush succeeded to the Babel of sounds, which he could not but have heard as he crossed the threshold. There was something ominous in that silence.

No need to ask if he knew. His face, pale as death, haggard, streaming with perspiration, proved all too plainly he was aware of the ghastly horror. But his first words, low, and uttered half unconsciously, were long after remembered :

" I wish I'd been found dead in that wood 'stead of Gibbs !"

Various circumstances arose, one after another, that united to surround George with a kind of network of suspicion. Simon Eade sustained himself like a man, with a proud confidence in the innocence of his boy, touching even those who could not share it ; and with a pious trust that Providence would yet see that innocence proved. But the poor feeble mother, shaken by ill health, half crazed by the remembrance of words and looks she would give the world to forget, could do little but weep, and utter broken supplications to Heaven.

George offered no resistance on his apprehension. Sternly, but without eagerness, he declared his innocence, and from that moment he kept entire silence. His features worked convulsively when he wrung his father's hand on parting, and gazed on the pale face of his mother, who had swooned away on seeing the police ; but he soon recovered his self-possession, and accompanied the officers with a steady step, and a fixed, though gloomy countenance.

The body of the deceased had been discovered about ten A.M. by a farmer going to the Plashetts, who had been attracted to the spot by the howls of Gibbs's dog. The corpse lay among the underwood, at a short distance from the footpath leading from the stile so often mentioned, through the wood to the Plashetts, and had apparently been dragged that short distance. Evidences of a fierce struggle were visible on and around the footpath, and some blood also : which appeared to have flowed from a wound in the back of the head of the deceased, who must have been struck from behind, by some heavy, though not blunt, instrument. When found, he had been dead, according to the medical testimony, some eleven or twelve hours. The pockets were turned inside out, and the watch and a purse had been taken, as well as a seal ring.

Gibbs's two servants, James and Bridget Williams, deposed that their master had quitted his own house on the night of the murder, at twenty minutes past eight, being unusually sober; that he had set his watch, the last thing, by the kitchen clock, and had observed that he should go to the Dunstan Arms first, and afterwards to the Plashetts. That his not returning that night had occasioned no uneasiness, as he was in the habit of frequently absenting himself until morning, and had his latch-key always with him.

On the other hand, Simon Eade, his wife, and servant girl, all deposed that George returned home on the night of the murder, at nine o'clock, having been out since tea-time; that there was nothing unusual in either his manner or appearance; that he supped, and afterwards remained with his parents till ten, when the whole family retired to bed; and that he came down next morning in the sight of Jemima, who had herself risen somewhat earlier than usual.

On his left wrist was found a recent cut, which he stated had been caused by his clasp-knife slipping, as he was cutting his bread and cheese. In the same manner he sought to account for certain marks of blood on the inside of his coat sleeves and on his trousers. The only article belonging to the deceased that was found in his possession was a small lead pencil, marked with the initials " G. G." and three notches; these Job Brettle, the blacksmith, swore Gibbs had handed him the pencil to cut, on the afternoon of the murder. He (Brettle) noticed both notches and initials at the time, and could swear that the pencil in the prisoner's possession was the pencil he had cut. George maintained that he had picked it up on the common, and that he had no idea to whom it belonged.

It came out in cross-examination that a more desperate quarrel than ever, had taken place on the morning of the murder, between Mr. and Mrs. Gibbs; after which, she had been heard to declare that she could support that life no longer, and would apply for help to one who would not refuse it. That she had sent a letter soon after to George Eade, by the son of a neighbouring cottager, and had gone out herself at night, a few minutes after her husband, returning again in a quarter of an hour, more or less, when she had retired to her bedroom, and had not again quitted it until news was brought next morning of the discovery of the corpse.

When questioned by the coroner as to where she had been overnight, no reply could be elicited from her; but she fainted so frequently while under examination, that her evidence was singularly broken and incoherent.

George admitted having gone to the Southanger Woods at about twenty minutes to eight on the night of the murder; but he refused to assign any special reason for going there, declaring that he had not remained there more than a quarter of an hour at most. He stated that, as he was re-crossing the stile, he saw Gibbs and his dog at a distance, making directly for it. The moon shone almost as bright as day, and he recognised him distinctly. To avoid meeting him, he took the Dring road, and walked nearly as far as the turnpike, when he turned about, and so reached home at nine o'clock without having met a soul.

The following were (briefly) the points in the prisoner's favour :

1. The evidence of three credible witnesses that he returned home at nine o'clock, and sat down to supper without any appearance of hurry or agitation.

2. The shortness of the time in which to commit such a deed, and effectually to conceal the property taken from the deceased.

3. The high moral character born by the prisoner up to that time.

The points against him were:

1. The cut on his wrist, and marks of blood on his clothes.

2. Gibbs's pencil, found upon him.

3. The absence of testimony corroborative of his own account of his doings during the thirty minutes that intervened between Gibbs's leaving the Dunstan Arms (where he had gone straight from home) and his (George's) own return to his father's.

4. The bitter animosity he was known to cherish against the deceased, and certain words he had been heard to utter respecting him, indicating a desire for his life.

By the evidence of the landlord of the Dunstan Arms, it appeared that Gibbs had left his place to proceed to the Plashetts, at a few minutes before half-past eight o'clock. Now, it would take some four or five minutes' moderate walking for one leaving the public-house, to reach the spot where Gibbs's body was found; thus reducing the period for the murder to be committed in (if committed by George at that time) to three or four and twenty minutes, if he ran home at his full speed, or to nineteen or twenty minutes, if he walked at an average pace.

The demeanour of the prisoner before the magistrates, was stern, and even defiant; but he betrayed no emotion. He was fully committed for trial at the approaching assizes.

Meanwhile, opinion respecting him was greatly divided in Cumner. He had never been a popular man, and his extreme reserve during the last three years had alienated many who, at the period of his great trouble, had been disposed to sympathise with him. And, although he had always held a high place in public estimation, the impression that he was a man of unusually fierce passions, and implacable resentment, had gained ground of late. In short, not a few of those who knew him best, believed that, worked up to savage fury by the sufferings of the woman he had once so fondly loved, and by long brooding over his own wrongs, he had revenged both himself and her by taking the life of his enemy. He might, it was thought, have easily slipped out of his father's house in the dead of night, have waylaid and murdered Gibbs as he was returning from the Plashetts, and have secreted or destroyed the property in order to throw suspicion off the right scent.

His trial will long be remembered in those parts, as well from the intense excitement it occasioned in that particular locality, as from the strong interest manifested about it throughout the kingdom. The most eminent counsel were engaged on his behalf; and Mr. Malcolmson, who never could believe in his guilt, spared neither pains nor expense to aid his cause. He was perfectly calm when he stood in the dock, the one object on which countless eyes were eagerly riveted; but the change that had taken place in his outward seeming, struck even the most indifferent beholder with compassion, and possibly did more to impress the jury in his favour, than even the eloquence of his counsel, wonderful

as that proved. For, his sufferings must have been intense. He had grown years older, during the last few weeks. His hair had thinned; his clothes hung upon his attenuated frame. He, once so ruddy and vigorous, stood there wan, haggard, drooping. Even the expression of his countenance had altered; it was stern no more.

A sound like one vast sobbing sigh went through the crowded court when the verdict, Not Guilty, was heard; but no applause, no public mark of joy or gratulation. And silently, with downcast eyes, like a doomed man, George Eade returned with one parent to the home where the other sat praying for his release.

It had been expected that, if acquitted, he would leave Cumner, and seek his fortunes elsewhere. But it was consistent with the character of the man, to brave the opinion of his fellows, and he did so in this instance. On the first Sunday, to the surprise of all, he made his appearance in church, sitting apart from the rest of the congregation, as though unwilling to obtrude himself upon them; from that time his attendance was invariable. Nor was this the only change observable in his conduct. His moroseness had passed away. He had become subdued, patient, manifesting a touching gratitude to those who treated him with common civility, as though he felt himself unworthy of their notice; unremitting in his devotion to his parents; working hard all the day; sometimes puzzling over a book at night; never alluding to the past—never forgetting it; melancholy —more melancholy than ever; but no longer bitter nor resentful. Such had George Eade become; and when men saw him at a distance, they followed him with their eyes, and asked one another in a whisper, "Did he do it?"

He and Susan never met. She long lay dangerously ill at her father's house, whither she had removed after the tragical event. And the old farmer was fitly punished for his sordid coveting of Gibbs's wealth, when it was found that the latter had settled only fifty pounds a year upon his wife, to be forfeited altogether if she should make a second marriage.

It was about a twelvemonth after these events that, one bright moonlight night, as Mr. Murray was sitting in his library alone, his servant entered to inform him that a stranger, who gave his name as Luke Williams, desired to speak with him. It was past ten o'clock, and the clergyman's hours were early and regular.

"Tell him to call to-morrow morning," said he; "this is not a fit hour for business."

"I did tell him so, sir," the man replied; "but he declared his was a business that would not wait an hour."

"Is he a beggar?"

"He didn't beg, sir; but he looks shocking, quite shocking——"

"Show him in."

The man entered; truly a shocking object. Pale, hollow-eyed, cadaverous, with a racking cough that caused him to pant and gasp for breath, he looked like one in the last stage of consumption. He gazed at Mr. Murray with a strange and mournful expression, and Mr. Murray gazed at him.

"Well?"

The stranger glanced at the servant.

"Leave the room, Robert."

Robert did so, but remained in close proximity outside.

"This is a strange hour at which to disturb me. Have you something to say?"

"It *is* a strange hour, sir, for coming; but my reason for coming is stranger."

The man turned to the window, the curtains of which were not drawn, and gazed at the full October moon, which lighted up the quaint old church hard by, the humble gravestones, the quiet home scene, and shed a solemn glory over all.

"Well?" Mr. Murray asked once more.

But the man's eyes were fixed on the sky.

"Yes," he said, shuddering, "it shone like that—like that—the night of the—murder. It did indeed. It shone on his face—Gibbs's—as he lay there—it shone on his open eyes—I couldn't get them to shut; do what I would, they would stare at me. I've never seen moonlight like that since, till to-night. And I'm come to give myself up to you. I always felt I should, and it's better done and over. Better over."

"You murdered Gibbs? You?"

"I did. I've been there to-night, to look at the place. I felt I must see it again; and I saw his eyes, as plain as I see you, open, with the moonlight shining on them. Ah, a horrible sight!"

"You look very wild and ill. Perhaps——"

"You doubt me. I wish *I* could doubt. See here."

With a trembling emaciated hand he drew from his pocket the watch, seal ring, and purse that had belonged to Gibbs; and laid them on the table. Mr. Murray knew them.

"I used the money," said the man, faintly. "There were but a few shillings, and I was in great want."

Then he sank down on a chair with a dreadful groan.

Mr. Murray gave him a restorative, and after a time he rallied. With his hollow eyes still gazing at the moonlight, and with that ever-recurring shudder, he faltered out at intervals the following story.

He and Gibbs had been formerly associated in disreputable money transactions, which had ended in his own ruin. Being in abject distress, he had, on the promise of a considerable bribe, agreed to aid Gibbs in a plot to obtain possession of Susan's person. When she and George had separated for the fortnight previous to their contemplated marriage, the two confederates had followed her to Ormiston, and, concealing themselves in a low part of the town, had kept close watch upon her movements. Ascertaining that she was to spend the day with a cousin, they sent a woman, a creature of their own, to waylay her on her road, with a message purporting to come from George Eade, imploring her to hasten to him immediately, as he was injured by an accident on the railroad, and might have but a few hours to live. Appalled by such intelligence, the poor girl hurried to the place where the woman led her, entered without a shadow of suspicion a lonely house in the suburbs, and found herself in the presence of Gibbs and Williams, who, instantly securing the door, informed her that this subterfuge had been resorted to in order to get her into the power of the former. They told her that she was now in a place where screams would not be heeded, even if heard, and whence she would find it impossible to escape, and that she would not be quitted night or day by them or their female assistant, until she should consent to become the wife of Gibbs. Who added, with furious oaths, that had her union with George Eade taken place, he would have shot him down on his way from church.

Wild with terror and astonishment, helpless, bewildered, the girl resisted longer than might have been expected in one naturally weak. But finding herself incessantly watched, trembling, too, for her life (for Gibbs stood over her with a loaded pistol and the most furious threats), she was frightened at last into writing, at his dictation, the letters to her aunt and lover, announcing her marriage; though that event did not really take place till nearly three weeks later, when, worn out, and almost stupified into acquiescence, she was married in due form. Even then, Williams declared that she would have resisted still, but for her fears for her lover's safety. His life seemed to be dearer to her than her own happiness, and Gibbs had sworn so vehemently that his life should be the immediate forfeit of his union with her, that she felt that union would be impossible. She married, therefore, offering herself up as a kind of ransom for the man she loved. Then Williams claimed his reward.

But his worthless confederate was not one to fulfil honestly any promise involving the sacrifice of money. He paid the first of three instalments agreed upon; but constantly shirked the payment of the others, until at last, Williams finding himself in immediate danger of arrest, made his way down to the neighbourhood of Cumner, and lurking about the Southanger Woods, the deep recesses of which were well calculated for concealment, watched his opportunity, and accosted Gibbs one evening as he was driving home from Tenelms alone. That worthy, though, as usual, half drunk, recognised him at once, and swearing at him for an impudent beggar, did his best to drive his horse over him. Infuriated by such treatment, Williams wrote him a letter, declaring that if he failed to bring, on a certain night to a certain spot in Southanger Woods, every shilling of the sum he had promised to pay, he (Williams) would the very next morning go before the nearest magistrate and reveal the whole plot of Susan's abduction and marriage.

Alarmed by this threat, Gibbs answered the appointment, but without bringing the money; indeed, it soon became clear that he had no more intention of paying it than before. Williams, exasperated beyond endurance by these repeated disappointments, and rendered desperate by want, swore he would at least possess himself of whatever money or valuables the other had about him. Gibbs resisted with fury, and a fierce struggle ensued, during which he repeatedly endeavoured to stab his opponent with his clasp-knife. At length Williams prevailed, and throwing all his strength into one supreme effort, hurled Gibbs to the ground, the back of whose head striking with fearful violence against a tree, he was killed by the force of the blow. Appalled by his own act, and by the probable consequences to himself, Williams hastily dragged the body from the footpath, rifled the pockets, and hurried away from the scene. The church clock struck ten as he emerged from Southanger Woods; he walked all that night, rested the next day in an old outhouse, and succeeded in reaching London undiscovered. But he was, almost immediately afterwards, arrested for debt, and had remained in prison until within the last few days, when he was released chiefly because he was believed to be dying of consumption. And he *was* dying, he added, despairingly. For, since that fearful night, the victim's upturned eyes had followed him everywhere—everywhere—and his life had been a burden to him.

Such was the tale, told in broken whispers in the dead of night, to the clergyman, by that miserable man: a tale impossible to doubt, and triumphantly proving the innocence of one who had been too long suspected. Before twelve o'clock next day, the whole village was ringing with the news of Williams's confession, which spread like wildfire.

George bore his triumph, as he had borne unjust suspicion. The man's character had been strangely purified in the furnace of that affliction. The awful fate of his enemy, overtaking him with the suddenness of a chastisement from Heaven, had struck George at the time with a strange compassion, as well as self-upbraiding. For, though guiltless of Gibbs's death, he was not guiltless of many and eager longings for it; and he would have given worlds to have forgiven him, as he hoped himself to be forgiven. Hence his first sad and self-accusing words in his father's house, after hearing of the murder.

It may be mentioned, by the way, that the object of the letter he had received from Susan on the morning of the fatal day, had been to implore him to call upon her father that very afternoon, and induce him to take immediate steps for effecting her separation from her husband, of whom she went in fear of her life, and by whom she was watched too closely to be able to assist herself. And as her letters were liable to be opened, she entreated George to meet her in Southanger Woods that night, in order to inform her of the result of his negotiation (which was never even entered into, as the farmer happened to be from home). Finding, however, that Gibbs was bound to the Plashetts from the public-house, she had rushed out hastily to warn George of the circumstance, and so prevent a meeting between the two, which was very near taking place.

Susan fully confirmed the testimony of Williams as to the circumstances of her abduction.

That wretched man survived his confession little more than a week, and died in prison, penitent.

And once more George and Susan met. At that interview he took from his bosom a little silken bag, in which was a bunch of withered hops, so dried by time, that they almost crumbled beneath his touch. And he held them up to her.

There is a cottage on Cumner Common, not far from Simon Eade's, the walls of which are covered with roses and clematis. There you may see Susan, if not as beautiful as of yore, still fair; and happy now, with her brown-eyed baby in her arms; and, if you choose your hour, you may catch George, too, coming in to dinner or to tea, stalwart, handsome, with a bright cheery look on his honest English face, that will do you good to look upon.

VIII.

TO BE TAKEN FOR LIFE.

Sophy read through the whole of the foregoing several times over, and I sat in my seat in the Library Cart (that's the name we give it) seeing her read, and I was as pleased and as proud as a Pug-Dog with his muzzle black-leaded for an evening party and his tail extra curled by machinery. Every item of my plan was crowned with success. Our reunited life was more than all that we had looked forward to. Content and joy went with us as the wheels of the two carts went round, and the same stopped with us when the two carts stopped.

But I had left something out of my calculations. Now, what had I left out? To help you to a guess, I'll say, a figure. Come. Make a guess, and guess right. Nought? No. Nine? No. Eight? No. Seven? No. Six? No. Five? No. Four? No. Three? No. Two? No. One? No. Now I'll tell you what I'll do with you. I'll say it's another sort of figure altogether. There. Why then, says you, it's a mortal figure. No nor yet a mortal figure. By such means you get yourself penned into a corner, and you can't help guessing a *im*mortal figure. That's about it. Why didn't you say so sooner?

Yes. It was a immortal figure that I had altogether left out of my calculations. Neither man's nor woman's, but a child's. Girl's, or boy's? Boy's. "I says the sparrow, with my bow and arrow." Now you have got it.

We were down at Lancaster, and I had done two nights' more than fair average business (though I cannot in honour recommend them as a quick audience) in the open square there, near the end of the street where Mr. Sly's King's Arms and Royal Hotel stands. Mim's travelling giant otherwise Pickleson happened at the self-same time to be a trying it on in the town. The genteel lay was adopted with him. No hint of a van. Green baize alcove leading up to Pickleson in a Auction Room. Printed poster "Free list suspended, with the exception of that proud boast of an enlightened country, a free press. Schools admitted by private arrangement. No-

I went to the Auction Room in question, and I found it entirely empty of everything but echoes and mouldiness, with the single exception of Pickleson on a piece of red drugget. This suited my purpose, as I wanted a private and confidential word with him, which was: "Pickleson. Owing much happiness to you, I put you in my will for a fypunnote; but, to save trouble here's fourpunten down, which may equally suit your views, and let us so conclude the transaction." Pickleson, who up to that remark had had the dejected appearance of a long Roman rushlight that couldn't anyhow get lighted, brightened up at his top extremity and made his acknowledgments in a way which (for him) was parliamentary eloquence. He likewise did add, that, having ceased to draw as a Roman, Mim had made proposals for his going in as a converted Indian Giant worked upon by The Dairyman's Daughter. This, Pickleson, having no acquaintance with the tract named after that young woman, and not being willing to couple gag with his serious views, had declined to do, thereby leading to words and the total stoppage of the unfortunate young man's beer. All of which, during the whole of the interview, was confirmed by the ferocious growling of Mim down below in the pay-place, which shook the giant like a leaf.

But what was to the present point in the remarks of the travelling giant otherwise Pickleson, was this: "Doctor Marigold"—I give his words without a hope of conweying their feebleness—"who is the strange young man that hangs about your carts?"—"The strange young man?" I gives him back, thinking that he meant her, and his languid circulation had dropped a syllable. "Doctor," he returns, with a pathos calculated to draw a tear from even a manly eye, "I am weak, but not so weak yet as that I don't know my words. I repeat them, Doctor. The strange young man." It then appeared that Pickleson being forced to stretch his legs (not that they wanted it) only at times when he couldn't be seen for nothing, to wit in the dead of the night and towards daybreak, had twice seen hanging about my carts, in that same town of Lancaster where I had been only two nights, this same unknown young man.

It put me rather out of sorts. What it meant as to particulars I no more foreboded then, than you forebode now, but it put me rather out of sorts. Howsoever, I made light of it to Pickleson, and I took leave of Pickleson advising him to spend his legacy in getting up his stamina, and to continue to stand by his religion. Towards morning I kept a look-out for the strange young man, and what was more—I saw the strange young man. He was well dressed and well looking. He loitered very nigh my carts, watching them like as if he was taking care of morning I looked out again, and there he was once more. I sent another hail after him, but as before he gave not the slightest sign of being anyways disturbed. This put a thought into my head. Acting on it, I watched him in different manners and at different times not necessary to enter into, till I found that this strange young man was deaf and dumb.

The discovery turned me over, because I knew that a part of that establishment where she had been, was allotted to young men (some of them well off), and I thought to myself "If she favours him, where am I, and where is all that I have worked and planned for?" Hoping—I must confess to the selfishness—that she might not favour him. I set myself to find out. At last I was by accident present at a meeting between them in the open air, looking on leaning behind a fir-tree without their knowing of it. It was a moving meeting for all the three parties concerned. I knew every syllable that passed between them, as well as they did. I listened with my eyes; which had come to be as quick and true with deaf and dumb conversation, as my ears with the talk of people that can speak. He was a going out to China as clerk in a merchant's house, which his father had been before him. He was in circumstances to keep a wife, and he wanted her to marry him and go along with him. She persisted, no. He asked if she didn't love him? Yes, she loved him dearly, dearly, but she could never disappoint her beloved good noble generous and I don't-know-what-all father (meaning me, the Cheap Jack in the sleeved waistcoat), and she would stay with him, Heaven bless him, though it was to break her heart! Then she cried most bitterly, and that made up my mind.

While my mind had been in an unsettled state about her favouring this young man, I had felt that unreasonable towards Pickleson, that it was well for him he had got his legacy down. For I often thought "If it hadn't been for this same weak-minded giant, I might never have come to trouble my head and wex my soul about the young man." But, once that I knew she loved him—once that I had seen her weep for him—it was a different thing. I made it right in my mind with Pickleson on the spot, and I shook myself together to do what was right by all.

She had left the young man by that time (for it took a few minutes to get me thoroughly well shook together), and the young man was leaning against another of the fir-trees—of which there was a cluster—with his face upon his arm. I touched him on the back. Looking up and seeing me, he says, in our deaf and dumb talk: "Do not be angry."

"I am not angry, good boy. I am your friend. Come with me."

I left him at the foot of the steps of the

Library Cart, and I went up alone. She was drying her eyes.

"You have been crying, my dear."

"Yes, father."

"Why?"

"A head-ache."

"Not a heart-ache?"

"I said a head-ache, father."

"Doctor Marigold must prescribe for that head-ache."

She took up the book of my Prescriptions, and held it up with a forced smile; but seeing me keep still and look earnest, she softly laid it down again, and her eyes were very attentive.

"The Prescription is not there, Sophy."

"Where is it?"

"Here, my dear."

I brought her young husband in, and I put her hand in his, and my only further words to both of them were these: "Doctor Marigold's last prescription. To be taken for life." After which I bolted.

When the wedding come off, I mounted a coat (blue, and bright buttons) for the first and last time in all my days, and I give Sophy away with my own hand. There were only us three and the gentleman who had had charge of her for those two years. I give the wedding dinner of four in the Library Cart. Pigeon pie, a leg of pickled pork, a pair of fowls, and suitable garden-stuff. The best of drinks. I give them a speech, and the gentlemen give us a speech, and all our jokes told, and the whole went off like a sky-rocket. In the course of the entertainment I explained to Sophy that I should keep the Library Cart as my living-cart when not upon the road, and that I should keep all her books for her just as they stood, till she come back to claim them. So she went to China with her young husband, and it was a parting sorrowful and heavy, and I got the boy I had another service, and so as of old when my child and wife were gone, I went plodding along alone, with my whip over my shoulder, at the old horse's head.

Sophy wrote me many letters, and I wrote her many letters. About the end of the first year she sent me one in an unsteady hand: "Dearest father, not a week ago I had a darling little daughter, but I am so well that they let me write these words to you. Dearest and best father, I hope my child may not be deaf and dumb, but I do not yet know." When I wrote back, I hinted the question; but as Sophy never answered that question, I felt it to be a sad one, and I never repeated it. For a long time our letters were regular, but then they got irregular through Sophy's husband being moved to another station, and through my being always on the move. But we were in one another's thoughts, I was equally sure, letters or no letters.

Five years, odd months, had gone since Sophy went away. I was still the King of the Cheap Jacks, and at a greater heighth of popularity than ever. I had had a first-rate autumn of it,

and on the twenty-third of December, one thousand eight hundred and sixty-four, I found myself at Uxbridge, Middlesex, clean sold out. So I jogged up to London with the old horse, light and easy, to have my Christmas-Eve and Christmas-Day alone by the fire in the Library Cart, and then to buy a regular new stock of goods all round, to sell 'em again and get the money.

I am a neat hand at cookery, and I'll tell you what I knocked up for my Christmas-Eve dinner in the Library Cart. I knocked up a beefsteak pudding for one, with two kidneys, a dozen oysters, and a couple of mushrooms, thrown in. It's a pudding to put a man in good humour with everything, except the two bottom buttons of his waistcoat. Having relished that pudding and cleared away, I turned the lamp low, and sat down by the light of the fire, watching it as it shone upon the backs of Sophy's books.

Sophy's books so brought up Sophy's self, that I saw her touching face quite plainly, before I dropped off dozing by the fire. This may be a reason why Sophy, with her deaf and dumb child in her arms, seemed to stand silent by me all through my nap. I was on the road, off the road, in all sorts of places, North and South and West and East, Winds liked best and winds liked least, Here and there and gone astray, Over the hills and far away, and still she stood silent by me, with her silent child in her arms. Even when I woke with a start, she seemed to vanish, as if she had stood by me in that very place only a single instant before.

I had started at a real sound, and the sound was on the steps of the cart. It was the light hurried tread of a child, coming clambering up. That tread of a child had once been so familiar to me, that for half a moment I believed I was a going to see a little ghost.

But the touch of a real child was laid upon the outer handle of the door, and the handle turned, and the door opened a little way, and a real child peeped in. A bright little comely girl with large dark eyes.

Looking full at me, the tiny creature took off her mite of a straw hat, and a quantity of dark curls fell all about her face. Then she opened her lips, and said in a pretty voice:

"Grandfather!"

"Ah my God!" I cries out. "She can speak!"

"Yes, dear grandfather. And I am to ask you whether there was ever any one that I remind you of?"

In a moment Sophy was round my neck as well as the child, and her husband was a wringing my hand with his face hid, and we all had to shake ourselves together before we could get over it. And when we did begin to get over it, and I saw the pretty child a talking, pleased and quick and eager and busy, to her mother, in the signs that I had first taught her mother, the happy and yet pitying tears fell rolling down my face.

THE END OF THE CHRISTMAS NUMBER FOR 1865.